I0731138

Trapped
In Love

DANICA FLYNN

TRAPPED IN LOVE

A MACGREGOR BROTHERS BREWING COMPANY BOOK

DANICA FLYNN

Trapped In Love

Copyright © 2022 Danica Flynn
This is a work of fiction. Names, characters, businesses, places, events, and
incidents are either products of the author's imagination or used in a
fictitious manner. Any resemblance to actual persons, living or dead, or
actual events is purely coincidental.

All rights reserved.

Ebook ISBN: 978-1-957494-02-9
Print ISBN: 978-1-957494-03-6

Cover Design: Emily's World of Design
Cover Photography: Eugene Partyzan & Angel Simon/ Deposit Photos
Editors: Leah Francic & Kate Seger

Content Note: Mentions of a parent with a drug addiction.

To all the messy girls who are the conductors of the hot mess express, I see you. And so does Gemma. LOL.

PLAYLIST

"Miss Take" By The Horrorpops
"Hate to Love You" By Karmin
"I Hate Everything About You" By Three Days Grace
"Who Invited You" By The Donnas
"I hate u, I love u" By Garrett Nash, Olivia O'Brien
"Do I want to know" By The Arctic Monkeys
"Take me to church" By Hozier
"Kiss This" By The Struts
"Girls Like Girls" By Hayley Kiyoko
"Baby Lou Tattoo" By The Horrorpops
"Summertime Sadness" By Lana Del Rey
"Time to Pretend" By MGMT
"Sweater Weather" By The Neighborhood
"Bad Guy" By Billie Eilish
"Girls/Girls/Boys" By Panic! At the Disco
"Under Pressure" By Queen/David Bowie
"Back To Black" By Amy Winehouse
"I knew You Were Trouble" By Taylor Swift

CHAPTER ONE

GEMMA

JUNE

I blinked and stared at my brothers-in-law while I processed what they had just asked me.

The MacGregor Brothers couldn't look more different, but they had similar mannerisms. While Declan rubbed a nervous hand across his clean-shaven jaw, his older brother Nolan mirrored the reaction by brushing his hand across his big, bushy beard.

"Well?" Nolan asked.

I blinked back at him. "That's the stupidest fucking name for a beer I've ever heard!"

Declan busted up laughing. "Told you!"

Nolan scowled, which was his usual MO anyway. Everyone knew Nolan MacGregor was the biggest grump in all of Drakesville.

I pinned him with a confused look. "Norah's Nectar, really? Nol, that sounds gross!"

Declan tried so hard not to laugh, while Nolan stood up and started pacing around the office. The pacing wasn't new. My sister was heavily pregnant, and the stress was getting to her husband. Lately, he was such a grumpy bear that everyone was walking on eggshells around him.

I got that he wanted to name the new hefeweizen after his baby, but Norah's Nectar was dumb as shit. I chewed on my lip and ran a hand down my tattooed arm as I tried to come up with a better name.

Immediately, a thought struck me.

"Ooh! I got it!" I cheered.

"What?" Nolan growled.

See — grumpy bear!

A smile curled up onto my lips. "Mac Daddy!"

Nolan frowned. "That's so stupid!"

"Nope!" Declan agreed with me. "I like it. It gets people to go 'whoa, what's that?' and pick it up."

"Exactly," I said. "This beer's new. It shows we're experimenting and trying new things. It should have a unique name."

Nolan gnashed his teeth, but then he nodded and walked out of the room.

Declan shrugged. We were all used to Nolan The Grouch by now. Declan went to say something else to me, but then his phone rang, and his brow furrowed in confusion. He held up a finger for me to wait before I darted back out to the serving floor.

"Gemma's coming to get you," he said into the phone.

My eyes widened. By his words, I knew exactly who he was talking to. Oh, shit, it was go-time. Avery was having the baby!

"Go," Declan said when he hung up the phone and

handed me the go-bag Nolan had stashed behind Declan's desk.

"I'm supposed to be on shift. Asher can't handle the bar himself tonight."

Declan swore. "Call Felix. Tell him it's an emergency."

I gritted my teeth and fingered the crystal around my neck. I tried to will away the bad vibes as I thought of Felix fricking Jameson.

I used to like Felix. A lot. He was funny and hot with his eyebrow piercing and sleeve tattoos. Back in January, he asked me out, but then he stood me up. If he apologized, I wouldn't have hated him with the passion of a thousand fiery suns. Instead, he pretended he never asked me out and said it was a joke.

What a douche-canoe.

The worst part? It absolutely crushed me. We had gotten close over the weeks leading up to our date, and my heart did that little pitter-patter every time he was near. Felix intrigued me, and I had wanted to get to know him better. I had hoped going out together, I'd find out more about him. I had already liked what I saw, so when he pretended I meant nothing, it broke my heart. Maybe it was typical 'Gemma Dramatics,' but the hurt of his betrayal rubbed me raw and turned into unbridled hatred.

Declan gave me a warning look. "Just call him."

"Can't you do it?"

While Nolan handled the beer, Declan managed the business side of the brewery. That included managing the front-of-house staff. It wasn't my job to call Felix to cover my shift. Same way, it shouldn't have been my job to handle the social media or work with Felix on the artwork, but Declan was an asshole like that.

"Just do it," he said.

Before I could argue, he rushed out of the office to get Nolan.

I sighed, pulled out my phone, and found Felix in my contact list. I clicked on the name 'Douche-Nugget.'

Felix standing me up wasn't the first time that happened to me. That's probably another reason it crushed my heart into a million tiny pieces when he did it. I'd used dating apps for a while, but if my matches didn't ghost me before scheduling a date, then they stood me up. Just like Felix. A part of me seriously wondered if Felix had cursed me because I hadn't been on a successful date since that night.

I pressed my phone to my ear and hoped the douche in question didn't pick up. I'd rather bother Wyatt or Claudia to come in instead of Felix.

But before I could hang up and call one of them instead, a gruff voice purred in my ear, "Well, hey sweet thing, what can I do for you?"

I rolled my eyes so hard I heard my sister in my head scolding me about my face staying that way. "Yeah. Never mind."

Felix chuckled on the other line. "Hold up now. What's up?"

"Avery's having the baby."

"Okay."

"Can you cover my shift tonight? I need to be with my sister."

I was met with silence for a couple of moments.

"Felix?"

"Yeah. I can do it. But you owe me."

I could only imagine what that meant. But he was doing me a favor, so I couldn't complain.

"K, bye!"

I hung up without another word. I didn't care if I was rude; he was an asshole and deserved it. I noticed Declan leaning against the doorway of the office, staring at me with an annoyed look on his face.

Declan seemed mild-mannered, but he was the most gossipy person at the brewery. He meddled. Wyatt and Lizzie wouldn't have ever gotten married if Declan hadn't pressed Wyatt about it. Nolan never would have told my sister he loved her if Declan hadn't pushed him to talk about his feelings. Okay, that last one was on me too, but Nolan was a special case. The big man would rather chew off his own hand than talk about feelings. Declan forced me to call Felix because he was urging me to bury the hatchet with the other bartender.

"Will you two get it over with already?" Declan asked.

"What?"

He shook his head and walked over to his desk. "Just fucking bang him already so the rest of us can have some peace. We're sick of your banter."

"When he stops being an asshole, maybe I will. I gotta go!"

I rushed out of the brewery and began walking to my apartment on the other side of town. Since Drakesville was so walkable, I never drove to work, but I needed my car to take my sister to the hospital. After Nolan knocked up my sister and moved her into his house, I offered to take over her place. It was a small second-floor apartment, but the rent was astronomically cheaper than what I paid in South Philly. I used to hate that the brewery was in the suburbs, but I'd come to love the small town of Drakesville.

I made the ten-minute walk to my apartment and hopped into my car for the thirty-second drive across the street to the high school. After parking, I jogged inside to find my sister sitting in her classroom, holding her back and groaning.

I never ever wanted to get pregnant. Ever. I couldn't wait to be the cool aunt to little Norah, but I didn't want to be anyone's mom. Ever.

Avery's eyes welled up with tears, and she clenched her teeth. "Nolan?"

I gave her a reassuring smile. "On the way. He'll meet us, okay?"

She nodded, but the color drained from her face. She gritted her teeth again as she pressed her hand onto the small of her back. "Fuck, I can't believe she's coming early."

I laughed. Of course, she was coming early. Norah was my sister's kid, after all. Avery was nothing if not a rule-following punctual lady. AKA the complete opposite of me. "She seems like your daughter already."

Avery glared at me through another grimace, and I took that as a sign to hustle her outside and into my car. Drakesville didn't have its own hospital, so it took ten minutes to drive to the nearest one.

I tried to calm my sister down, but she was freaking out for the entire ride. I opened my center console and pulled out a moonstone necklace, and handed it to her.

She tilted her head at me. "What's this?"

Avery didn't get my belief in crystals. I tried to give her some when she was dealing with morning sickness, but she scoffed at me and called it 'woo-woo bullshit.' Whether or not they worked, they helped me put out good vibes into the universe.

"It's a moonstone," I explained.

"Is this some woo woo bullshit?"

I rolled my eyes, although I wasn't shocked in the least by her comment. "Avs, just take it and channel your stress into it until we get to the hospital. I promise you, as soon as we get there, Nolan will whisk you away and hold your hand the entire time."

"Thank you."

"I know you don't believe in this stuff—"

She cut me off. "I know you do it because you want to help. I love that you do that, even though I think crystals are bullshit."

I nodded and pulled up at the hospital. Just like I said, Nolan met us immediately. He rushed to my car and opened the passenger door to help Avery. He had her wheeled into the hospital before I could even put my car in park. I drove around the lot, searching for a parking spot while trying not to worry about my sister.

I messed up early in Avery's pregnancy when she thought something was wrong with the baby and she couldn't get a hold of me. I was supposed to meet her for dinner, but I was spiraling after Felix stood me up. I flaked out on her and fell asleep with a dead phone, so I never saw her pleading texts until it was too late. I never told her what happened because I felt so guilty about not being there for her. Since then, I had been trying to make amends.

After parking and walking into the hospital, I found Declan and my dad sitting impatiently in the waiting room. We sat for hours while Nolan was in the room with Avery. I paced so much that Declan had to push me down into my seat. Avery had been so afraid of something happening to the baby her whole pregnancy that I wanted the birth to be perfect.

I rubbed at my rose quartz necklace and tried to put happy thoughts into the universe for little Norah. I wanted my niece to be brought into the world surrounded by love.

"She's gonna be fine," Dad reassured me.

"She was scared," I admitted.

"She's got, Nol. You're not the one giving birth," Declan said.

I nodded in agreement, but I still wished I could be by Avery's side. Nolan was holding her hand and telling her everything was all right, but I needed my sister to be okay.

It was late by the time Nolan came out, looking exhausted but with a big grin across his face.

I jumped up at the sight of him. "Can we see them?"

He nodded, and we all followed him into the room, where Avery lay in the bed with the baby in her arms. She looked wrecked, but wore the same happy smile on her face as when she married Nolan.

"Oh my god, she's so cute," I squealed.

Nolan glared at me.

"What?" I asked him.

"Be quiet. She's fussing," he said in a low growl.

Man, was little Norah going to have it hard as a kid. Nolan was going to be a total helicopter parent.

But then I watched Avery hand the baby over to him, and Nolan's entire demeanor changed. The baby wrapped a tiny hand around his finger, and the big guy was glowing.

Holy shit, Nolan had feelings!

"You good?" I asked my sister.

She nodded and handed me back the moonstone necklace, but I shook my head and pushed it back into her hand. "Keep it."

I made that necklace a while ago, but I wasn't sure when to give it to her. The universe gave me the sign today when she was freaking out.

We stayed visiting, watching my dad rock the baby, until she wailed uncontrollably.

"All right, get out!" Nolan said to all of us.

Avery and I laughed together, and I hugged her goodbye.

"Thanks for being here," she said and squeezed my hand.

"Of course. I can't wait to spoil Norah rotten."

She smiled at me. "Love ya, sis."

"Love ya, too. I'm so happy for you."

Tears pricked her eyes. "I never thought I'd get everything I ever wanted with Nolan."

I wiped her tears away. "The big guy loves you something fierce. Never ever forget that."

She nodded and watched as Nolan rocked the baby, trying to calm her down.

As I was leaving, I glanced at Avery and Nolan one last time. I'd never seen either of them look happier before. I had to tamp down the jealousy boiling to the surface. I hoped one day I could find my person like my sister had. If only Felix Jameson hadn't cursed me.

CHAPTER TWO

FELIX

*a*sher pinned me with a confused look as I walked behind the bar and put on my apron.

"I thought you switched with Gemma?" he asked while filling a glass with Drakesville Lager for a customer.

I shook my head. "No, I was covering her shift last night. The three of us were always scheduled tonight."

I wasn't supposed to work last night, and it ruined my movie night plans with my little sister, Skye. We planned to celebrate the start of her summer vacation like we always did, but I couldn't say no when Gemma told me Avery was having the baby.

Family meant everything to me, and it was the reason Gemma thought I was an asshole. Despite the absolute dick-hole behavior I showed to Gemma, I was a nice guy at my core. So, of course, I covered her shift. Being an asshole to her was just a front. I wasn't gonna tell her, 'Sorry, Gemma, I stood you up because my dad's in jail, and I have custody of my little sister again.' It was better if she hated me instead.

"Gemma needed a favor," I explained.

Asher's eyebrows rose up high. "And you said yes?"

Okay, *maybe* my fights with Gemma were well documented. I'd rather she hated me than pitied me, though. Even if it sucked working beside the pink-haired hottie all the time. Was it a good plan? Absolutely not. But I didn't want her to know about my fucked up childhood.

"Avery had the baby. I couldn't say no when Gemma needed her shift covered," I explained.

Asher pursed his lips, but left his comment unsaid when some customers came up to the bar, and we got busy serving them beer.

A couple of minutes later, I saw a flash of pink in my periphery.

Gemma.

I silently cursed and walked to the other end of the bar to clear away empty beer glasses. It was better if Gemma and I kept a few feet of distance between us.

"Hey, Gem," Asher greeted.

I glanced over at the statuesque tattooed beauty as she clocked in for her shift. My eyes dipped down her frame and traced the lines of the flower tattoos on her arm. Chicks with tattoos and unnaturally colored hair were my weakness. With her pink hair and tattoos, she made my dick stand at attention, but I couldn't go there. Not when I had slammed that door shut earlier this year.

Her blue eyes shot up to me when she caught me staring, and then the standard 'Gemma Scowl' marred her pretty face. "Take a picture. It will last longer," she snapped.

"What are you in the fifth grade?" I teased.

Asher sighed. "I don't know why Dec puts you on the schedule together."

Asher walked into the back office, probably to bitch about us to Declan. It wouldn't have been the first time.

I knew why Declan put Gemma and me on the same shifts. The same reason he forced me to work with her on the artwork for the brewery instead of doing it himself. He already told me to bang it out to give the rest of them a break. Yeah, no. If I got one taste of Gemma Jensen, I'd never let her go. But I'd only disappoint her in the end when I chose my sister over her.

Gemma was still glaring at me, but her next retort died on her lips when a guy wearing a Philadelphia Bulldogs jersey sat down. Gemma put on her customer service smile and leaned against the bar.

"What can I get you?" she asked.

"Are you on the menu?" hockey-bro joked.

I rolled my eyes, but Gemma gave the douche a flirtatious laugh. She had that way about her. She radiated positivity, and when she smiled, it was like the warm rays of the sun shone down on you. She never smiled at me like that. Instead, I got the heated glare of a woman scorned.

"No can do, my friend!" she told the customer with a laugh.

The guy laughed with her. "I'll take the 611 Ale."

"Ooh, great choice. I love that one!" Gemma said as she poured him the beer. She caught me staring at her. "What are you looking at?" she hissed in a whisper.

"Just you, sweet thing."

She rolled her eyes. "Christ, does that work on other women? So cheesy. Get out of my face, Felix."

I smirked and walked over to her, pretending I was

doing something behind the bar. I bent down to her ear. "You want to see how good it works?"

I swore I felt her shiver, but then she shoved me away. "That ship sailed a long time ago."

She handed the beer over to her customer, and I'd be lying if I said I didn't watch her sweet ass as she walked away. It was a little fun to rile her up.

A familiar voice pulled me from my thoughts—one I had no desire to hear ever again. The blood drained from my face when I came face-to-face with my ex, Roger.

Roger looked freshly shaven and was wearing a tailored suit, which looked amazing on him. Why did he look that good? And who wore a suit to a freaking brewery? Beside him was a pretty blonde woman with cat-eye glasses.

"Hey, what are you drinking tonight?" I asked, pretending to play it cool.

"Hey Felix, you still working in this dump?" he asked. The blonde cringed and gave me an apologetic look.

"You mean this awesome brewery with amazing beer?" Gemma cut in.

I side-eyed her. I didn't know why she was coming to my rescue. Why would Gemma, of all people, want to help me?

Gemma put on that bright smile again. "Felix, take a break. I'll handle this."

"You sure?" I asked.

"Yeah, I just took mine. Go on."

We both knew it was a lie. What was she playing at?

I stared at her awkwardly for a second, and she nodded toward the kitchen. I didn't wait for her to change her mind. I walked away, hoping to get some air. I also hoped Gemma didn't ask me what that was about.

I wasn't 'out' per se. I didn't care who knew I was bi. I

just couldn't handle the bi-erasure of people asking if I was 'sure' or the pitying looks when they told me it was 'okay to be gay.' Of course, it was, but being bisexual was different. I hated explaining that shit to people.

I found my buddy Ryan in the back alley, smoking a cigarette. "Hey, man," Ryan greeted me.

Ryan used to work behind the bar, but now he helped Nolan and Allen brew the beer. He said working under Nolan was tough because the big guy was a micromanager. That didn't surprise me, because Nolan could be a grump. But his attention to detail made the MacGregor Brothers Brewing Company so successful.

Nolan was great for advice, too. Over the years, I'd gone to him for help. He sympathized with my situation with my sister, since his parents died when he was eighteen, and he had become a parent at a young age. I even told him about my breakup with Roger. Instead of asking me about my sexuality, he said, 'Here, try this new beer I'm working on.' I liked Nolan for that. He might be a grumpy asshole, but you could trust him with anything.

I sighed. "Hey."

Ryan narrowed his eyes at me. "What's up?"

"Fucking Roger's here."

His dark eyes widened, and he ran a golden-brown hand across his stubble uncomfortably. Ryan knew I was bi because we had been best friends since I was three years old. That's the kind of friendship you had in a town like Drakesville. He knew all my secrets, and I knew his.

"Why?" he asked.

I shrugged. "No clue."

He stubbed out his cig. "So what, you ran away?"

I leaned against the wall. "Nah. Gemma told me to go on break."

"Man, you two need to stop fighting. Just tell her about Skye, and fuck her already," he said with a grin. He thrust his hips out, acting like he was humping the air.

I rolled my eyes at him. "Nah, that ship has sailed, man."

I felt my phone buzz in my pocket and saw a text from my sister.

HALF PINT: *Can I stay at Sophia's tonight?*

ME: *Did you do your chores?*

HALF PINT: *FE-FE! It's SATURDAY. I'll finish them tomorrow.*

I sighed. This single dad thing was no joke. I was trying to do the best for Skye, but she definitely had me wrapped around her little finger.

I typed back a response.

ME: *Promise?*

HALF PINT: *Yes! You're the best big bro! See you tomorrow!*

I sighed and shoved my phone back into my pocket. Ryan arched a dark eyebrow at me. "Skye," I explained.

He nodded. "You gotta be firm with her, dude. That's the only way kids learn. Skye needs structure."

"I know. She's gonna be at your sister's house."

Sophia was Ryan's niece, so I knew Skye was always in excellent hands with Ryan's sister, Christine.

"Still, dude, you let her get away with everything."

I nodded. Ryan was right, but I didn't care right now. The selfish part of me was glad I had a night to myself. I didn't get many of those lately, so I might as well enjoy it.

CHAPTER THREE

GEMMA

I lifted the last chair and stacked it on the table while I hazarded a glance at Felix across the room. Since that rude guy showed up, he had been quiet, almost muted. His energy was off, and bad vibes had radiated off of him all night. I tried to shake off my empathic nature because Felix damn sure didn't deserve my pity.

I just wanted to close the bar without further arguments. I told Asher to take off already, since there wasn't much more to get done. Declan had already left as well. He didn't hang around because he knew Felix and I could manage closing. Felix was wiping down the countertops, but I still needed to vacuum the floor.

I walked back toward the supply closet to grab the vacuum. When I turned around to walk out, Felix stood in front of me, almost menacingly, that I nearly jumped out of my skin.

"Fuck! You scared the shit out of me!"

"Sorry," he muttered, giving me an uncharacteristic look of apology.

"What do you want?" I growled and tried to muscle my way out of the closet, but I tripped over my own feet and would have landed on the floor if he hadn't put a steady hand on my hip.

My breath caught in my throat at the weight of his hand. My sex-deprived brain couldn't stop thinking about what his hands could do to me. Images of his tattooed arm slipping down between my legs and inside my underwear flashed inside my mind.

I really need to get laid.

He took his hand off me, and I found myself disappointed. I shouldn't have felt that way. I should have shoved him off me and told him to get bent.

He took the vacuum out of my hand. "There's not much left to do. You can go home if you want."

I shook my head. "Nah, you can't close by yourself."

"Okay, in that case, sweet thing, get your fine ass out there and help me close up."

"You're insufferable," I said with a scoff and gave him the signature 'Gemma Glare' he was used to. Most people didn't get that look. I prided myself on being a beacon of positivity, but with Felix, I let all my negative energy bubble to the surface. It wasn't healthy, and I didn't like that about myself, but he brought out the worst in me.

"You love it," he teased.

"I hate you. Get out of my face."

"No, you don't," he said. He reached a hand up and pushed a strand of my hair behind my ear. I shivered at his touch, and hated myself for it.

"Yes. I do," I argued, but my voice faltered. He didn't

move his hand, instead he framed my face, forcing me to look into those dark eyes of his.

"You love our banter," he said, almost seductively. He stared intently at my lips like he was thinking of leaning down and kissing me.

"Banter? I can't stand you!" I exclaimed and fixed him with another glare.

But he smirked at me, like the cat who got the cream. Like he was about to do something that was really going to piss me off.

Before I could stop him, his lips descended on mine. I should have pushed him away, but my hormones got the better of me, and I melted into his kiss. His tongue slid across my lips, and his hands went into my hair, pulling me closer. I moaned and opened to him, letting him angle my head into whatever position he wanted.

He kissed me like a man starved, and it made my body come alive. Maybe that was why I didn't stop him. Not when his hands roamed down my body or when he gripped my ass. And certainly not when he shoved me up against the wall.

What did I do instead? I wrapped my legs around his waist and moaned into his mouth. I snaked my hands through his hair and gripped his shaggy locks while he deepened the kiss. He nipped at my lip. Oh god, I felt the hard weight of him against my leg, and I wanted more. I wanted to feel all of him pressing deep inside me.

His beard tickled my skin as his lips traveled down my jaw and kissed the side of my neck. "Gemma," he whispered in my ear.

As soon as his lips left mine, the spell broke, and I remembered why I hated him. Even if my horny brain didn't want him to stop.

"Why did you do that?" I asked, finally snapping out of it.

"Because you looked like you needed to be kissed. And it was the only way to shut you up," he explained in a husky whisper against my neck.

"Asshole!"

"You want me to stop, sweet thing?" he purred in my ear while pressing small, teasing kisses below my ear.

"No," I moaned before I could stop myself.

Yes. I wanted him to stop. I wanted him to stop before I dropped to my knees and sucked him off in the supply closet. Before I made 'bad Gemma decisions' and slept with my arch-nemesis. I needed him to stop before he put his spell on me again.

But rational Gemma wasn't in charge. Horny Gemma was. And horny Gemma didn't give a fuck how Felix had wronged us.

"No, sweet thing?"

"Please?" I begged and arched my hips up, waiting for him to plunge a thick digit between my legs.

"No."

"What?" I asked in disbelief and sighed when he set me back down on my feet.

"Not like this."

"Because you don't want me?" I cried.

Of course, he didn't want me. He only kissed me so he could reject me again. Because that was the kind of asshole he was. Tears threatened as I realized I had fallen for his bullshit once again. I couldn't let this douche-canoe see how much his rejection crushed me. How once again, he fooled me.

Felix twirled a strand of my pink hair around a finger. "I'm not fucking you in the supply closet. I want to bend you over my bed and take you from behind while I grip your pretty hair in my fist."

Ohhh.

"You want that, sweet thing? You want me to press you into the mattress as I have my way with you?"

I whimpered.

Yes, yes, I did. I wanted all of that. And more. I wanted him to choke me while he told me I was a naughty girl.

This was a bad idea on so many levels, but horny Gemma had taken over, and she didn't care. Not one bit. The only thing she cared about was getting underneath this tattooed hottie as soon as possible.

"Let's finish closing up and then I'll take you home and wrap my mouth around your clit, huh, sweet thing?"

I must have been drunk on his kisses because I nodded instead of telling him to go fuck himself. Felix threaded his hands through my hair when he kissed me one last time, nice and slow, like he was savoring me. Like he was promising me what would come later if I behaved myself. But I didn't want to be good. I wanted to misbehave so badly that he punished me for it.

I opened my eyes when he pulled away, and his dark eyes bored into me. Then his lips turned up into a mischievous smile. "The quicker we finish tonight, the quicker I'll have you coming, okay, sweet thing?" he purred.

I didn't know why I nodded and agreed with him. I shouldn't be doing this, but I was horny with a capital H.

"Wait, I want to know one thing," I said.

"What's that?" he asked.

His eyes were still dark with desire. He wanted me as badly as I wanted him. Dec was right. Maybe Felix and I needed to bang it out. If we got all our aggression out in the bedroom, we wouldn't bring it to work anymore. That would have made Declan happy, since he threatened to write us up after our last fight. He didn't give a damn if I was family. He was serious about making sure the brewery wasn't a hostile working environment.

"Who was that guy tonight?" I asked.

Felix's eyes narrowed, and he looked pissed off.

Felix was a dick, but he never looked furious at me before. The look that marred his face was scary.

He ran his tattooed hand down his face. "Gem, I don't want to talk about my ex."

Oh.

Ohhh.

Wait a second.

"Wait, are you gay? Is that why you stood me up? If that was the case, that's totally fine." I held up my wrist. On it was a heart filled with block colors of pink, purple, and blue, depicting the bi pride flag. "I'm a loud and proud Bi girl, but I'm confused because you—"

He slanted his mouth on mine again, silencing my confused questions. When he pulled away, he pressed my hand against his raging boner. "Definitely not gay, or you wouldn't do this to me. I'm bi too. I hate that I'm expected to 'come out' when straight people don't have to do that shit."

"Oh. Okay, I get that. Your secret's safe with me."

He grinned. "It better be, or I might have to spank you."

I gave him a cheeky grin. "Don't threaten me with a good time."

"Oh, yeah?" he asked and raised his pierced eyebrow.

"We're gonna do a bad job closing, aren't we?" I asked with a laugh.

"Let's get it done, so I can taste your cum on my tongue."

I whimpered a little at that.

"Now, Gemma," he snarled and gave me a light tap on the ass. He didn't have to tell me twice. I practically raced out of the supply closet to do the quickest closing possible.

☀

"Oh, fuuuckkk," I moaned as Felix's vibrating tongue ring hit the perfect spot on my clit.

Yes, the man had a vibrating tongue ring he carried around with him. And holy shit, he was good at eating pussy.

"That's it, come for me, sweet thing," he purred when he lifted his head up from between my legs.

After we did the worst closing I'd ever done in my life, we went back to my place since it was closer. I'd get an earful from Declan about it, since it was unlike both of us. But I didn't care because Felix had a VIBRATING tongue ring, and he was using it on me. His tongue ring was enough to make oral interesting, but I gasped out loud when he turned it on in the middle of going down on me. It made me wonder what other sorts of toys he had.

Focus, Gemma! This is a one-time thing!

Watching his tattooed arm slip down between my legs while he pressed two fingers inside my pussy had been the hottest thing I'd ever seen. I arched my hips off the bed, pressing myself further into his mouth. I cried out as my spine tingled, and I came all over his face.

It took me a couple of seconds to come back down to earth. When I opened my eyes, he looked up at me with a satisfied smirk across his bearded face. He turned off his tongue ring but pressed small kisses on my thighs.

"Good, sweet thing?" he asked.

"Good?" I repeated, panting as I came down from my high.

He grinned. "No? Was it bad? Let me try again. You can sit on my face this time and ride my beard until you cream all over it."

I whimpered. God, I wanted that, but I felt bad I hadn't touched his dick yet. I wanted to choke on it while he fucked my face.

"I want to suck your cock," I panted out.

"Yeah, you do," he said with a cocky grin.

He got up from the bed, and I watched him undress. Felix didn't have six-pack abs or big muscles, but I've never been into guys with muscles as big as my head. He was on the lanky side, but with those piercings and tattoos, I was a goner.

I gave him my best seductive smile as I crawled over to him. I looked up at him with innocent eyes, and I stroked his rock-hard cock.

He reached a hand down and rubbed his thumb across my bottom lip. "Wrap these pretty lips around my cock, sweet thing."

I stroked along his shaft teasingly, then I bent down to lick around the head.

Felix gripped my hair. "Now, Gemma."

"Make me."

"Such a brat," he joked, and then he bucked his hips and forced his dick into my mouth. I moaned and rolled my tongue around his length. I opened my mouth wider as I took him deeper.

He bucked his hips. "That's it, you take it all."

I moaned on his cock as he fucked my face, and I did as he commanded.

"Good girl."

He thrust his hips to push his dick deeper into my mouth, and I took him as far into my throat as I could. I swirled my tongue and sucked until he hit my gag reflex. I slid a hand down to fondle his balls, but then he wrenched his cock out of my mouth.

"Did I do something wrong?" I asked as I sat back on my haunches. I wiped at my mouth and then my eyes because choking on his dick made my eyes water. But I loved it. I loved being a brat and being punished by getting face-fucked. Until I was a wet, sloppy mess.

He rubbed his thumb across my swollen lips. "No, sweet thing. I love what this mouth can do, but I'd rather come in your pussy. Okay?"

I nodded.

He started calling me 'sweet thing' at the brewery to annoy me. But in bed, I liked the pet name. Way too much than I wanted to admit, especially to myself.

He pushed me onto my back and crawled into the bed with me. He cupped my face as he kissed me gently.

"Please, Felix," I begged when his lips traveled down my neck.

"You want me, huh?"

I nodded.

He grabbed a condom from my nightstand, took it out of the packaging, and slid it down his length. My mouth hung open when he found the lube in my nightstand and slicked it down his cock. Dudes never thought of that! It was nice when someone was considerate in bed.

I gasped when he flipped me over so I was on all fours and gave my ass a little smack.

"You brat, I know you like that," he said into my ear.

I smiled to myself and was glad he couldn't see the satisfied look on my face. He teased me with the head of his cock against my clit, and I arched back into him, desperate to get him inside me.

He gave me another slap on my ass. "Be patient."

"Or what?" I asked.

"Or you won't get my dick at all."

"Please, I need it."

He circled the head of his cock around my clit, torturing me by not giving me what I wanted. "You need it, huh?"

"Please."

"You'll be good now? Or does the little brat need a spanking?"

I bit my lip as images of me against his lap and his hand smacking across my ass popped into my head. I wanted to see his tattooed arms swinging down in the air until a loud crack sounded across my skin. Until he made my ass cheeks red and raw because I was a naughty girl who needed to be punished.

I jolted when he slapped his hand across my ass again. "Huh, sweet thing? You want me to press you face-down against the bed and spank you? Or do you want my cock?"

"Cock!" I exclaimed. "Please."

"Good girl," he purred. He tilted my head back toward him and kissed me while he pressed inside me nice and slow.

He broke our kiss as he set the pace, sliding in and out in a slow rhythm.

I groaned and gripped the sheets in front of me.

"You feel so good," he moaned in my ear as he moved inside me.

I didn't want slow. I wanted to get fucking railed. I ground my ass back into him, and he seemed to get the hint by the way he curled his fist around my hair. I felt a tingle on my scalp, but pain turned to pleasure when he quickened his pace and took me hard.

"Yes, right there," I moaned.

"Take it," he growled in my ear. He pulled my hair harder and slapped my ass again. I wanted him to choke me too, but I only did that with someone I trusted completely.

"I am," I moaned back at him. My vision swam in front of me as my orgasm coursed through me. Wave after wave washed over my body. "Give me more."

Tonight was a 'Gemma makes bad decisions' night, but I didn't care when his cock felt so good inside me. I was never supposed to sleep with him. Not after he stood me up and never explained himself. Not when, overnight, he turned into the biggest jerk in all of Drakesville. But I was weak for a tattooed man.

He gripped my hair even tighter, and his thrusts got more erratic. He took me faster and harder, and I let him. I loved the way he manhandled me and held me down against the mattress while he fucked like he could go all night.

"You better fucking come," he said into my hair.

"I already did."

The grip on my hair tightened. "Again, Gemma. Don't make me tell you again. Come on my cock."

I nodded into the bed, and then he reached around and found my clit. That set me off.

"FELIX! Fuck, fuck, fuck, fuck," I cried out into my pillow and slumped face-down onto the bed in pure bliss.

"I'm gonna come," he whispered into my ear.

He turned my head toward him and kissed me through his orgasm. His cock twitched inside me, and I took it as we kissed until we were both finally spent.

I slumped against the bed, out of breath and feeling like my body was made of jelly.

He brushed my hair off my shoulder and pressed a gentle kiss on my skin. He massaged my scalp for a couple of seconds before he pulled out. It was sweet of him to give me a little aftercare, but I wasn't naïve. I knew I'd wake up alone tomorrow.

CHAPTER FOUR

FELIX

I ran my hand through Gemma's cotton-candy pink hair as she lay sprawled across my chest. I wanted to enjoy this quiet moment together as we lay entwined, but I had to leave. I couldn't let her think this was anything more than a one-night stand.

Gemma turned on her side, and I thought she had fallen asleep until I heard her bedside drawer creak open. My dick lifted up in interest, thinking she was ready for round two, but then she turned back to me and thrust a reddish-brown stone at me.

"What's that?" I asked.

"Jasper. It helps with stress. I can feel it rolling off of you."

I furrowed my brow. I knew Gemma was eccentric, but I didn't know she actually believed in healing crystals. She wore a pink crystal around her neck all the time, and I only noticed it because it rested against her tits, and she constantly fidgeted with it.

"Gem, you don't seriously believe in this stuff?" I asked.

She fingered the pendant at her neck. "Sure I do! It helps me put good vibes into the universe. Your aura has been off since your ex showed up."

My aura? What the fuck was she talking about?

She shoved the stone at me again. "Just do it!"

I took it from her and rubbed my fingers against the smooth stone. I don't think it did anything, but I took it to appease the hot, naked lady beside me.

She lay back down and cuddled into my side. A smile upturned on my lips, and I wrapped an arm around her. It was nice having someone to cuddle, but this was only for tonight. I would cut and run once she fell asleep. I would make her hate me even more than she already did. At least I learned what Gemma tasted like and what sounds she made when she came all over my dick.

"Christ," she swore.

"What?"

She laughed and skimmed a hand down my torso until she gripped my dick. "How are you hard again?"

I gave her a wink. "That's what you do to me, sweet thing."

She rolled her eyes, but then she bent over and took me in her mouth again. Well, if I was going to make her hate me again, at least I'd make tonight count.

☀

I woke to birds chirping and the blinding sensation of sunlight shining down on me. It was like mother earth slapping me in the face for the evil deeds of last night. I slid my eyes open and swore under my breath when I realized I never went home.

Gemma's lithe body was curled into my side like she belonged there. Her tattooed arm laid across my chest and her palm was flat against my heart while her hair fanned out over my shoulder. I wanted so badly to stay right here in her bed, holding her in my arms like we belonged together. But I didn't have time for a relationship, and I couldn't let her get any ideas about us.

I shifted her onto her back, and she stirred but didn't wake. I slid out of her bed. I found my clothes, crumpled them into a ball, and tip-toed out of her bedroom. I closed the door gently to not wake her and got dressed in her bathroom. Gemma's apartment was hot as balls. I hadn't noticed last night because she had the window unit A/C running in her bedroom all night.

I checked my phone and sighed when I saw it was dead. It was a dick move, leaving without saying goodbye, but I had to do it. Gemma already hated me and thought I was an asshole. I might as well convince her of that even further.

I quietly let myself out of her apartment and walked the couple of blocks to my house. The twin home I lived in with my little sister wasn't mine, even though I had been paying the mortgage since Mom left when I was fourteen. Dad's drug habit got worse after Mom left. He was never abusive, but Mom couldn't handle his addiction. Rather than get him help, she left. Leaving me to raise my baby sister.

For the past couple of years, Dad had been getting better. He even talked about trying to go to rehab again. That was why I asked Gemma out back in January. I felt like I could finally commit to a relationship. Then Dad got arrested for possession again. It was like the universe told me I had to choose between my family or my love life. I would always choose my sister.

I walked up the steps and put my key into the lock, but

frowned when I discovered the door unlocked. The hair on the back of my neck rose in suspicion. I always locked the door.

I stepped inside and froze when I saw my little sister sitting on the couch, hugging her knees to her chest with tears streaming down her face.

Fuck.

"Half pint, what's wrong?" I asked.

"Felix?" she asked. "I came home, and you weren't here. Why weren't you here?"

I shouldn't have stayed at Gemma's. I didn't regret my night spent with her, but this was why I couldn't have a relationship. I couldn't let my sister down like our parents did.

I sat on the couch next to Skye and pulled her into my arms. "I thought you stayed at Sophia's? I'm here, half pint. I'm always here."

"I thought you left me," she blubbered.

My heart ached at her words. I never wanted her to feel abandoned.

"Skye, I went to a friend's and lost track of time. I didn't leave you. I'm here."

She wiped her eyes. "I'm sorry."

I ruffled her hair. "Nothing to be sorry about. I'm sorry I wasn't home."

She squinted up at me and stared at my neck. "Ooh."

"Oh, what?" I asked.

Her lips curled up into a smile. "You went to a 'special' friend's house."

"What?"

She pointed at my neck. "You have a hickey!"

Shit.

I rubbed the back of my neck. "How do you know what that is?"

She glared at me. "I'm not a child!"

Except she was. I tried to give her the birds and bees talk two years ago, and she told me the school had already given it to her, and she had the internet.

"Skye, don't let anyone give you hickeys. Not until you're thirty!" I joked.

She slapped my arm. "Stop it!"

"You okay?" I asked.

She nodded. "I'm sorry."

"I know."

She kicked my foot. "So who was it?"

"Nunya."

She rolled her eyes at the stupid dad joke I tried to set up. Then she frowned, and that put my 'dad senses' on high alert. "Felix?"

"Yeah, kiddo?"

"You don't have to be a monk," she said. She wrapped her arms around her knees and looked down at the floor. "You should have a life. A S-E-X life."

I covered my ears with my hands. "You're too young for that. Let's not talk about that." I wiped my hands on my jeans and stood up from the couch. "Did you have breakfast at Sophia's?"

"No. I left early," she said but didn't explain further.

Hmm. If there was anything I knew about teenage girls, it was to let them tell you when they were ready. I wouldn't pry, but I could tell something was up between my sister and her bestie.

"You want to go to the diner?" I asked.

"Which one?"

"Old York Grille. Come on, I'll buy you that fancy French toast."

Her brown eyes lit up. "The kind with Fruity Pebbles on it?"

I pointed at her. "That's the one. Come on, half pint, let your big bro treat ya."

She jumped up and hugged me. "You're the best brother ever!"

I smiled and ruffled her hair. "Your only one."

Skye went to the bathroom to wash her face, and I plugged in my phone while I waited for her. A slew of text messages popped up all at once. My heart broke at all the ones from Skye. I hated that she thought I had abandoned her. I knew the deep betrayal of coming home and finding the person you loved the most had packed their bags and left you.

"Let's go!" Skye cheered when she got out of the bathroom.

I smiled at her when she skipped outside.

It didn't matter if I wanted something more with Gemma. Skye was the most important thing in my life, and she would always come before anyone else. I'd only disappoint Gemma in the end. It was better this way.

CHAPTER FIVE

GEMMA

I wasn't surprised when I woke up alone and cold in my bed. That was partly because Felix ducked out early this morning, and partly because my A/C unit was running on full blast. I was disappointed but not shocked when he slipped out this morning when he thought I was asleep without saying goodbye. I wished it hadn't hurt my feelings, but it did. He could have at least stayed for breakfast. I wasn't so clingy that I thought last night meant anything. I knew it was a one-night stand.

I sighed and ran a frustrated hand down my face. Sleeping with Felix had been a mistake, but I didn't regret the way he played my body or made me come so hard I saw stars.

I grabbed my phone off my nightstand and checked my messages. I cringed at one from Declan.

DEC: *Dude, what happened last night? You and Felix did the worst job closing. I expect better of you.*

I expected better of me too. I should have never

succumbed to my desires last night. I shouldn't have let Felix kiss me in the supply closet. But my brain hadn't been in charge.

With another sigh, I crawled out of bed and took a shower, hoping to scrub the scent of Felix off my body. I got dressed and made the ten-minute walk over to Avery and Nolan's house. Avery was supposed to come home from the hospital tomorrow, and I was sure Nolan hadn't left her side yet. I wanted to clean up, so she and Nolan didn't have to worry when they brought the baby home.

The house was dark when I crept inside with my spare key, and it was obvious Nolan never made it home last night. Of course not. He was glued to Avery's side. It was cute how my sister made the big grouch show his soft, gooey center.

When I found out he got my sister pregnant, I thought it was the universe's way of forcing them to talk about their feelings. I had hoped for years they would see what was right in front of them. Before she got pregnant, I had no clue Avery had been sleeping with him. I thought they were friends who were totally clueless about how in love they were. The baby gave them the push to realize how perfect they were for each other, and I was glad to see my big sister find what she had always been searching for.

I started cleaning the house, then I made Mom's lasagna and stuck it in the fridge for Nolan to eat when he got home.

I was only eight when Mom died, so I didn't remember her much, but Avery forced me to learn some of her recipes. Avery kept Mom's memory alive through her cooking, but I didn't feel that connection to the woman we lost. That made me feel guilty, but I couldn't help that I barely remembered her. Not like it mattered all that much since

Avery mom-ed me pretty much my whole life after her death. She did it because Dad would have let me run around feral. Avery's words, not mine.

After cleaning up the mess I made in the kitchen, I started the laundry. My sister and her husband wouldn't want to do chores when they brought Norah home. Once the clothes were in the washer, I went upstairs into the nursery. I placed a rose quartz on the windowsill so it would be in direct sunlight. Avery could get mad at me about that later, but I wanted my niece to have love energy around her.

Normally, I didn't come over to do chores for my sister, but I still felt bad I wasn't there when Avery needed me when she was pregnant. I never told her what had been going on or the reason I hated Felix. She had so much going on with the baby and Nolan that I didn't want to bother her with my drama.

I startled at the sound of the front door opening downstairs, and then Nolan's thunderous footsteps pounded up the steps. He walked into the nursery and jumped when he saw me.

"Christ, kiddo, what are you doing here?" he asked, with that permanent scowl etched across his face.

"Wanted to clean, so Avery didn't have to bother when she brought Norah home. Why do you look so grumpy?"

He sighed and ran a hand through his thick beard. "Avery kicked me out because I was hovering. And I'm not letting her lift a finger when I bring her home tomorrow!"

I laughed. Nolan was so soft for my sister. "Don't hover, Nol!"

"She said I was annoying her. Thanks for helping, though. I know Avs appreciates it."

I nodded.

"Oh, hey!"

"What's up?"

His smile cracked his face, and I loved that my sister was the only one who got him to smile like that. "She agreed to name the beer Mac Daddy."

It had surprised me he asked Avery for her input on the beer name, but it was an awesome name. I sighed when I realized I had to talk to Felix about the art direction for the labels. It wasn't part of my job as a bartender, but since I handled the social media, Declan had me work with Felix on the artwork.

"What's wrong?" Nolan asked.

"I have to tell Felix what art to do for the bottles."

Nolan furrowed his brow. "How's that your job?"

I shrugged. "Declan makes me do it."

"Dude, he really wants you to be the marketing director."

I clenched my hands into fists and gritted my teeth. "But I don't want to!"

Nolan scowled again. "But we shouldn't be paying you for one job when you're doing two!"

I shook my head. "Don't worry about it, Nol. Is Avery taking visitors, or did you annoy her too much?"

He shook his head. "She's wiped out. Peanut was up all night. Come over tomorrow after we bring her home."

I smiled at the nickname he had for the baby. Nolan puffed out his barreled chest in pride when he talked about her.

"Okay, I'll call beforehand. I don't want to be in the way."

"You won't. Avs still needs you, okay?"

"Okay," I said in a quiet voice, but I didn't believe him. Avery didn't need me when she had him. It was me who needed her.

"You at the brewery tonight?" he asked.

I shook my head. "Nah. I'm not on the schedule."

He nodded. "Thanks for coming over and doing that stuff, Gem. I know your sister will appreciate it. I appreciate it too."

I gave him a cheeky grin. "Aw, Nol, ya big softie."

"You're a pain in the ass, but you're *our* pain in the ass," he grumbled.

"I better go," I said. "There's food in the fridge."

He furrowed his brow.

"It's not poison!" I joked. "I'm not as good of a cook as Avs, but I can still make our mom's lasagna."

Nolan grunted at me, which was standard operating procedure for the big guy. I laughed as I walked out of the house and toward my apartment on the other side of town.

I wanted to see my sister, and a part of me wanted to tell her what happened between me and Felix. But the other part didn't want to tell a single soul I slept with him. If I pretended it didn't happen, my heart wouldn't feel so heavy with grief. I felt so foolish for letting him into my bed.

If it was supposed to only be a one-night stand, why did my heart feel like he broke it again? I should have never let my horny brain control me last night. How was I going to work side-by-side with him now that he knew what sounds I made when I came?

That asshole would probably make snarky retorts about it too.

I was such a fool.

I walked up the steps inside my apartment in a huff, annoyed with myself for the mistake I made last night. The heat wafted toward me as I walked into my bedroom. I immediately shut the door and cranked the A/C to full blast before flopping down on my bed in defeat.

I should have done my laundry at Avery's. I wanted to wash the memory of Felix off my sheets and forget our night together. Forget that I let my guard down with him. Even if he had given me more orgasms than anyone else had in a long time. He was still a dick.

I sighed and pulled out my phone to text him about the artwork, even though I didn't want to.

ME: *We have a name for the hefeweizen. Mac Daddy.*

I sent him a picture of Nolan and Norah I took yesterday.

FELIX: *On it. I'll make him look like a lumberjack.*

I caught myself laughing out loud to myself.

That was perfect for my big and bearded brother-in-law. Avery said she loved his 'lumbersexual' physique, so she'd love it too. I wasn't sure if she realized Nolan made the hefeweizen for her. Just like he made that pumpkin beer for her last fall. He was already talking about making a wheat beer for her at Christmas, too. He claimed it was to bring in more beer drinkers that didn't like IPAs, but we all knew it was a lie. He did it all for Avery.

I glanced down at my phone and saw the dots blinking as if Felix was typing another message to me, but then they disappeared. I guess we were gonna pretend last night never happened. That was fine with me. It made it easier for me to continue hating him.

CHAPTER SIX

FELIX

*W*as I dick for pretending I never slept with Gemma? One thousand percent. Did it suck working beside her when she hated me even more than she already had before? Also, yes. But I had too much on my plate with Skye, and I couldn't give Gemma what she wanted.

Sleeping together solved nothing. In fact, it made the friction between us worse. She looked like she wanted to stab me daily. I tried my best to stay out of her way, but sometimes I couldn't help but fight back.

I wiped down the bar and slyly watched Gemma's ass as she flirted with the men at the other end of the bar.

"Dude, you gotta stop," Ryan said from the other side of the bar.

"Stop, what?" I asked, feigning unawareness.

I didn't have to tell Ryan what happened between me and Gemma. The first shift after we slept together, he saw how she glared at me more angrily than normal. Ryan kept trying to convince me that just because I was Skye's guardian didn't mean I shouldn't have a sex life. But he didn't have kids. He didn't get it.

"Dude, you know. You'd think it would have relaxed you at least," he muttered.

I raised my pierced eyebrow at him. "What do you mean?"

"Man, you need a vacation."

True. I needed a vacation a decade ago, but I didn't have the money to go anywhere.

I wanted to argue with him further, but then Avery MacGregor came up to the bar with her newborn strapped to her chest.

"Hey, Avs. How are you?" I asked.

"Tired," she said with a long sigh.

"Felix, go away. Let me talk to my sister," Gemma said from behind me.

I jumped at her voice because I hadn't heard her sneak up on me.

Avery rocked her crying baby. "Sorry to bring her in here, but she misses her daddy, and I can't get her to sleep."

"I'll get Nolan," I said.

"He's doing inventory," Ryan said. "I'll get him."

Avery rocked the baby in her arms, but the little girl wanted to cry to her heart's content. Avery looked like she either wanted to cry too or chug a beer. This was the first time I'd seen her since she had the baby a couple of weeks ago. I wasn't sure if she was breastfeeding, so I didn't want to offer her a beer if she still couldn't drink.

"Move," Gemma said to me as she set down a bottle of Mac Daddy on the bar in front of Avery. "Avs, can I take a picture of you and the baby? For our social media."

"Nolan should be in it," Avery said.

Avery looked exhausted and defeated by the baby's continued cries. Skye was two when Mom left, but I remembered those days. After my dad shut down and I had to raise my sister, I knew I had no desire to have kids of my own. That shit was hard. When people said stay-at-home parents didn't have jobs, I wanted to punch them. Raising kids was freaking hard.

"Felix, fuck off," Gemma said when she noticed I was still standing next to her.

"Gemma! Don't be so rude, and don't swear in front of the baby," Avery scolded her.

Gemma rolled her eyes, and I crossed my arms over my chest. "Are you done?" I asked.

"No! You're such a fucking dick. Get out of my face," she seethed at me, balling her hands into angry fists at her sides.

Avery sighed. "Can you two not start? I can't handle a crying baby and you fighting. Nol mentioned it's gotten worse between you somehow."

Yeah, I knew why it had gotten worse, and it was one hundred percent my fault. It surprised me Gemma hadn't told her sister why. The Jensen Sisters were close. Nolan mentioned he found out more about Gemma than he cared to know after marrying Avery.

"Ask your sister," I said over my shoulder as I walked to the other end of the bar to help a new group of patrons.

I served the customers their beers, but out of the corner of my eye, I saw Nolan walk out onto the floor. He grumbled at Gemma, but when he saw Avery, his entire demeanor changed. Whatever stress he walked in with faded away when he saw his wife and baby. He kissed Avery and bent down to kiss his baby's head. Nolan was the grouchiest asshole I'd ever met, but not with Avery. It was awe-inspiring how the petite woman brought him to his knees.

I watched Gemma take a few photos of the couple until Nolan got annoyed with her. She scurried away, probably to ask Declan for his approval on the postings for social media. Declan cut me a separate check for my designs whenever we had a new beer, but I wasn't sure he was doing the same for Gemma. That was shitty if she wasn't getting paid for all the extra stuff she did outside her role as a bartender. I shouldn't care about that, but I did.

"You look stressed," Avery said to me as I refilled her glass of water between customers.

The baby had stopped crying now that she was strapped to Nolan's chest. Huh. His wife was right. The baby was a daddy's girl. It was cute to see the big gruff guy melt at the sight of his tiny daughter.

"He needs a vacation," Ryan said, taking a swig of his beer.

I threw a rag at him. I didn't need my boss to know that.

"Dude, if you need time, talk to Declan," Nolan said. "We know how hard you work."

I shrugged. "I can't really afford to go anywhere."

"Oh!" Avery said, and her eyes lit up with excitement. "My dad has a cabin in the Poconos. You could totally go!"

I stared at her. "Really?"

She nodded. "It's not in the middle of nowhere, if that's what you're thinking. It's on a big resort lake, but it's beautiful. Think about it and let me know."

"It's a nice place, too," Nolan said. "That's where we went for our honeymoon."

I rubbed a hand across my beard. The idea was appealing. Getting away from town could be fun. And I could take

Skye with me. I'd still have to spend money I didn't want to, but it wouldn't be a lot, mostly gas and supplies.

I saw a flash of pink in my peripheral. If I left town, I'd have an entire week where I didn't have to endure Gemma's glares and snappy retorts. It would have been a welcomed break.

"I gotta talk to Declan about the schedule. I'll get back to you," I said to Avery.

She gave me a big smile. "No one's using it this summer. It shouldn't be a problem."

I knocked on Declan's open office door after closing down the bar for the night. He looked up at the noise. "Hey, man. You about to leave?"

I nodded and took a seat in the chair across from his desk. "Hey, can we talk about me taking some time off?"

"Man, I'd thought you'd never ask! You're just as bad as me and Nol."

"It doesn't matter when. I'm looking to take a week sometime this summer. Avery offered her dad's cabin in the Poconos, so it'd be nice to get away for a little."

He eyed me like he was calculating something silently in his head. "Actually, I'm hiring some help for the summer, so I can shuffle around the schedule. Dude, you work so hard for us. You deserve a break."

His words surprised me. I didn't know we were looking for more staff. We had a lot of college kids come back during the summer, so we were usually full up.

Declan pulled something up on his computer. "I have you on the schedule this week, but I could shift things around to give you next week off."

"Really?"

He nodded. "Yeah, man. Nol already told me you were gonna ask, so I've been messing around with the schedule."

"Okay, man, that would be great."

He pinned me with a hard look. "Maybe if you get out of town for a while, Gemma will get over whatever the hell you did to piss her off again."

I cringed. Declan had already reprimanded us for a loud fight we got into yesterday. I didn't blame him for that, it was unprofessional. Some breweries had toxic work environments, and Declan had been very clear about not having that here. He was a good boss, and I felt bad I put him in a tough situation.

I ran a hand through my beard and sighed. "Yeah, man, maybe."

"Get out of here and plan your vacation. I'll see you tomorrow."

I nodded and stood up to walk out. Gemma had already left, and I was glad I didn't have to run into her before leaving. Closing together had been a challenge because she snapped at me the whole time. Not like I didn't deserve it.

When I got home, I saw Skye's light was still on. It was the summer, so I gave her a bit of free rein, but it was still way past her bedtime.

I knocked on the door and waited for a response. I tried to respect her privacy as much as possible.

"Come in!" she called out.

I opened the door and saw her sitting up in bed, reading a book. She looked like Mom at that moment. Some days, I wished Mom had taken Skye with her. Skye barely remembered Mom, and Dad had been so absent her whole life that I was the only parent she'd ever known.

I sat on the bed. "It's past your bedtime."

She held up the book. "Good book."

"Okay, but don't stay up too late."

"How was work?" she asked.

"Good. But I want to ask you something."

"Yeah?"

"What if we went to the Poconos next week?"

She shook her head. "I'm going down the shore with Sophia and her family."

Right, I had forgotten about that. Skye always spent a week in Cape May with the Parks for summer vacation. They had been doing it since she was nine. When Skye was younger and still needed a babysitter, Ryan's sister, Christine, always helped and never let me pay her. She did it out of the kindness of her heart. I'm not sure I'd have survived single parenthood without the Parks.

"Why the Poconos?" she asked.

"Everyone's telling me to take a vacation. Nolan's wife, Avery, said I could use her dad's cabin up there."

"Fe-fe, you should go! You need a break."

I furrowed my brow. "What do you know about that?"

Skye set her phone down and bit her lip. "I know how much you sacrificed for me. Since Mom abandoned us and Dad...well, you know, you never got to be a kid. You've taken care of me my whole life."

I rubbed a hand through my beard. "Half pint, you're my whole world. I'll do anything for you. It's kind of the deal."

She shook her head. "I'm not a baby anymore. And I know you broke up with Roger because of me."

I cringed. I had hoped she didn't know that. Roger said I didn't have time for him, but we had other issues too.

I hated that I had to 'come out' to straight people, but it didn't matter to me who knew I was bi. Roger wasn't out.

He was too afraid to tell his uptight WASPy family he had a boyfriend, and he wanted to hide our relationship. My dad wasn't a bad guy, he was losing a battle with addiction, and I sympathized with his struggles. When I told him I liked men, women, and gender non-conforming people, he said, 'Who fucking cares? Love whomever you want, and don't let other people tell you it's wrong.' He might have been a shitty dad, but at least he wasn't a homophobe.

"That's between me and Roger. Nothing to do with you. Okay, half pint?"

She nodded. "Okay, but you should still take a vacation."

I smirked at her. "Okay, boss lady, I'll do that."

She laughed. "I'm not the boss. You are!"

I laughed with her and ruffled her hair. "Okay, kiddo. If I'm the boss, get to bed."

"Love you, butthead," she teased and hugged me.

I hugged her back. "I love you too, fart breath."

I got up from the bed and shut the door behind me before walking into my room. I took a quick shower, and after getting out, I checked my email to see what was in my queue for my freelance design work.

When I started working at the brewery, Declan noticed me drawing on a break and asked me if I'd ever consider redesigning the beer labels. They had outsourced someone to do it when they first opened and hadn't been happy with the results. I designed all my tattoos and was a self-taught graphic designer, so I never considered it something I could do for a paycheck. Declan and Nolan believed in me and gave me the freedom to work on my art. They had even encouraged me when I told them I was thinking about trying to get other work for it. Declan, being the jack-of-all-trades he was, coded my website for me, and told me I could use my brewery designs to start my portfolio. I'd done some logos for softball teams, authors, and a bunch of bars. I even did my first book cover last year.

I had one job in my queue that I was about to finish up, but I had nothing else lined up. Unless Nolan was working on adding more beers, but that wasn't likely until the fall.

Avery said the cabin had internet, so if I did have jobs come up while I was away, I could work on them. Just in case, I changed my availability on my website to closed and started researching the area where the cabin was.

It would be nice to get away for a while. I could do solo hiking and relax there. Maybe take my paints and work on my art for fun instead of a paycheck. Skye was safe with the Parks down the shore. Everything would be okay while I was gone. Maybe I could actually enjoy myself for once.

CHAPTER SEVEN

GEMMA

I walked into the brewery but stopped dead in my tracks when I saw three bartenders. Felix, Asher, and a blonde girl I'd never met before were behind the bar, taking care of customers. That didn't seem right. I was supposed to be on tonight. Declan mentioned getting more wait staff this summer, so maybe the unknown blonde was just shadowing the guys.

I walked over to the bar and put on my apron when Felix glanced at me in confusion. "What?" I snapped at him.

Yeah... I might still be mad that he cut and ran after we had sex. I might have been an extra bitch to him because of it. I'd admit, it was immature of me, but I was hurt. I knew it had been a one-night stand, but I didn't know he would leave without saying goodbye. That made me feel like garbage. I shouldn't have been surprised, since he had already shown his true colors, but I fell for his charm and the way he made me feel when his lips were on mine.

I tried to move on and forget about the night we spent together. But I was still struggling with all the dating apps. I'd gotten ghosted a couple times since that night, and I had another date bail. Safe to say, I was still convinced Felix cursed me. I had been charging my crystals more than ever, trying to put out my positive energy into the universe, but it wasn't working.

Anytime I saw Felix, rage bubbled up inside me. I wasn't myself around him. I held in all that negative energy and expelled it onto him. It wasn't good, but he made me so mad, I couldn't help myself.

Felix still had his pierced eyebrow raised at me. "You're not on the schedule."

I stared at him, unblinking as his words settled on me. That couldn't be right.

"What?"

"You're not supposed to work tonight."

He had to be mistaken. I always worked Wednesday nights, and the weekends, too. Declan always gave me the good shifts.

I squeezed my eyes shut and sighed.

Declan.

Of course.

He really wanted me to be the marketing director. He was doing this to punish me.

I walked past the bar toward Declan's office in the back. His office door was closed, but my eyes narrowed as I stared at the printout of the schedule hanging up on the wall outside. I wasn't on the schedule tonight, or tomorrow, or at all this weekend. That had to be a mistake. It just had to be. I glanced down to next week, and I had no shifts on the schedule either. Zero. That wasn't right.

I swung open the door and stormed into the office.

Declan sat behind his computer typing away, and he barely looked up at the commotion I made.

"You're not on the schedule," he said, never once taking his eyes off his screen.

"No, I'm not. What the fuck?"

He gestured to the seat in front of his desk. I took it but bounced my knees up and down to keep myself from exploding. Declan steepled his hands over his clean-shaven face. "I want you to take the marketing director position."

I leaned my head back and groaned.

"Come on, Gemma."

"Why are you pushing this? I already said no."

He gave me a hard look and started counting off on his hand. "One, I can pay you more. Two, you're good at this shit. And three, I'm the boss, so if I want to promote you, I'm gonna do it."

"So you're punishing me by not giving me hours?"

He sighed. "I'm still gonna pay you. I know you work twenty-four seven on the social channels. And you manage Felix with getting the art done in time. That's not your job as a bartender. I don't ask that of Wyatt, or Claudia, or even Asher. I only trust you."

"But I don't want this."

He ran a hand through his short-cropped brown hair. "Gem, stop being a pain in my ass. You have so many great ideas—the collaboration with the tattoo shop and selling beer at the tree lighting ceremony. You planned Avery and Nolan's wedding up in the loft and then helped us rent that space for events. This is what you should be doing."

Planning Avery and Nolan's quickie Christmas wedding had been fun. I got to decorate the loft upstairs like a Christmas winter wonderland. I even made a Christmas-style flower crown for Avery to wear instead of a veil. I surprised them both by having the staff set up brunch before they went on their honeymoon. It had been stressful, but I had a lot of fun doing it.

Declan was right, I was good at event planning, but the idea of being the sole person responsible for marketing for the brewery gave me hives. Anxiety built up inside me, just thinking about all the pressure that would be on me. I didn't want to have another mental breakdown like I did with my last marketing position. I'd rather stay behind the bar and give Declan my input when he asked.

"I like serving beer and engaging with the customers," I said.

All true. But still not the real reason I didn't want the job.

"When was the last time you went on vacation?" he asked.

I gave him a quizzical look. What did that have to do with the marketing director position?

I hadn't taken a vacation in several years. Since Declan hired me at the brewery, all I did was work and pick up extra shifts because I always needed the money. When I lived on South Street, I was barely getting by because my rent had been so expensive on top of the gas for my commute. That was why I jumped at moving into Avery's apartment when she moved in with Nolan.

"Not for a while. Why?" I asked.

"Look, take time off. I hired more help to free up the schedule. I want you to think hard about your future. Being a bartender's fun and all, but if you're not thinking of your five-year-plan, your career isn't going anywhere."

I didn't want to go anywhere. I loved working for the brewery.

He held up a hand before I could argue. "I want you to

think about your career here at the brewery. It's unfair for me to ask so much of you when it's not in your job description. I want you as my right hand. Nolan's shit at business. I need someone who likes to do stuff I don't give a fuck about."

"Fine," I spat and glared at him. "It was a real dick move taking me off the schedule."

"It was the only way I'd get you to listen. I'm serious about you spending time away from the brewery and thinking about it. You could use a vacation. Go down the shore or something. Okay?"

I rolled my eyes at him. "Fine."

I left the office in a huff, pissed that I was losing my hours because my boss thought he knew what I wanted out of my career better than I did.

I walked behind the bar, tore off my apron, and clocked myself out. Declan would pay me for the time I spent dealing with his bullshit meddling.

Felix gave me a curious glance while he filled a beer from the tap. "Everything okay?" he asked.

I glared at him. "Like you care."

"Gemma, I'm—"

"Save it. I'm outta here."

Was I being a dick to him? Yes. Did he deserve it? Absolutely.

I wanted a beer, but if I stayed at the brewery to drink one, we'd get into another screaming match. Instead, I stormed out and walked over to my sister's house. I was seeing red, but I needed her to help me be rational about this. Maybe I should quit. That would really show Declan.

Avery opened the door, and as soon as she saw the anguish on my face, she pulled me into a big hug. I leaned into the hug, bending down because my sister was short. I got Dad's height and lanky frame, while Avery was a little curvy and petite like Mom had been. I only knew that from photographs because I didn't remember Mom. I only thought about Mom when I made her lasagna or when it rained. When it stormed so hard, lightning shone through the entire night sky; it reminded me of the worst day of my life.

Avery sat me down at her kitchen table, and then I burst into tears.

"Oh, sis, what's wrong?" she asked.

I wiped my eyes. "Shit. Avs, I'm sorry. I didn't mean to come crying to you like I always do."

She reached across the table, grabbed a box of tissues, and handed it to me. "I know, but I'm always here for you. What's going on?"

I dabbed at my eyes. "Declan wants me to go on vacation."

She squinted at me, her gaze clouding with confusion. "Okay. That's good, right?"

"No. He cut all my hours for the next two weeks. He wants me to be the marketing director, but I don't want to!"

I cringed when I realized how loud my voice got toward the end of my sentence. Especially when a loud cry sounded from the other room.

"Don't get up. I got her!" I heard Nolan yell from the living room.

I cocked my head at my sister when I heard a Bulldogs hockey game turn on in the living room. It had to be an old game because I swore I heard the announcer mention Claude LaVoie with the puck. LaVoie might be the head coach for the team now, but he had hung up his skates a long time ago.

She shook her head but smiled big. "Norah and Nolan

are napping on the couch. She seems to only fall back to sleep if we put on hockey. There was an old game on the hockey network the other night, so Nolan recorded it for her."

I laughed. My family were such hardcore hockey fans; of course my little niece would already love the sport. "Shut up! She's so your daughter."

Avery laughed. "She so is. Dad will be disappointed if she doesn't like hockey. Hopefully that doesn't change when she gets older. Anyway, Nol's got the baby, so why don't you tell me what's up? All of it, Gemma."

"Felix cursed me!" I blurted out.

She raised an eyebrow and got up out of her seat. She walked over to the fridge, looked inside, and pulled out a beer. When she walked back over to the kitchen table, she handed me a 611 Ale. "You need a drink. Now, back that up and explain everything."

I took a swig of the beer and ran my fingers across the rose quartz pendant at my neck. "Everything's a mess. Declan wants me to think about my future and be his marketing counterpart."

Avery put a hand on her chin as she listened to me. "What does that have to do with Felix?"

I curled and uncurled my hands into fists as I thought about Felix. "He cursed me!"

I could tell she was trying to hold in her laughter. I believed so hard in the fate of the universe, but my sister didn't believe in it. She laughed at me, both to my face and behind my back, about it.

"How?" she asked gently, trying to appease my eccentricities.

I took another swig of my beer. "Do you know why I hate him?"

She shook her head.

I ran a hand down my face. "He stood me up."

Avery cocked her head at me. "He what?"

"He asked me out and didn't show up."

She peered at me suspiciously. "When was that?"

I frowned and looked down at my hands in my lap.

"Is that why you weren't around when I thought something was wrong with the baby?" she asked.

I nodded solemnly. "I'm sorry. That was the day after he stood me up, and he acted like it was a joke. Now, I can't seem to get a date, and I slept with him!"

Avery held up her hands. "Wait a second, backup. You slept with him? When?"

I grimaced. "When you had the baby. I've been on the apps and not making headway. If they don't ghost me, they stand me up. Felix cursed me, and now I can't find love, and I hate him so much. And I don't want to be the fucking marketing director!" I spewed it all out in a rush.

Nolan walked into the kitchen, rocking Norah in his arms. Avery smiled up at her husband, and he kissed her temple. He cocked an eyebrow at me. "You want me to talk to Dec? I told him not to cut your hours."

"No," Avery cut in. "I'm glad Declan did this."

I glared at her. "You're supposed to be on my side!"

"I *am* on your side. Do you want to be a bartender forever?"

"There's nothing wrong with being a bartender," Nolan said to her.

Avery shook her head. "I'm not saying there is, but, Gemma, you're so talented at event planning. And you're already doing the job Declan's asking you to do."

I frowned. "I don't want it to be like last time."

She gave me a sympathetic smile. Avery had been there

when I had the mental breakdown that caused me to quit my high-pressure corporate marketing job.

It had been too much stress, and I cracked underneath it all. It didn't help that I felt like I was constantly gaslit by my boss. She'd tell me to do something, and when I did what she asked, she'd claim it wasn't what we talked about. When it was one hundred percent what we talked about. The corporate world was hell, and I hated every minute.

Avery reached over and squeezed my hand. "It won't be like last time. Because you'll be the one in charge."

She was wrong. I couldn't handle the weight Declan was putting on my shoulders.

"It's too much to handle," I insisted. "Dec told me to go on vacation and think about what I want."

Nolan rocked Norah in his arms. "Not a bad idea, kiddo. You work your ass off for us."

I rolled my eyes at his kiddo comment. I was twenty-five; I wasn't a little kid.

"Oh, I know!" Avery said, with an odd twinkle in her eye. "Go up to the cabin."

Nolan furrowed his brow at my sister. "But isn't—"

Avery cut a glare at her husband, and Nolan clamped his mouth shut, but he still looked confused.

"Gemma, you love going up to the cabin during the summer!" Avery exclaimed. "You can go fishing and hiking and do all that boring outdoorsy stuff you like. If Declan took you off the schedule, it's perfect timing."

I loved going up to the cabin. I spent so many summers there with Dad after Mom died. I hadn't gone in a couple of years since I've been working non-stop at the brewery. Maybe it wasn't a bad idea to go to the cabin. Declan and Avery were right. I could use a vacation.

"Have a fun summer vacation up on the lake! It's totally

fine. Dad and Uncle Bill aren't up there right now. Summers on the lake were always fun for you," my sister tried to convince me.

I should have been suspicious of Nolan furrowing his brow at Avery like she had three heads. Or paid attention to the way she glared at him. But I was coming around to the idea of going to the cabin for a little R & R. Our cabin was in a wooded area that faced out onto the big lake. We even had our own dock for the kayak. It wasn't unusual for me to take a solo fishing trip up there, either. I just hadn't done it in a while.

Maybe it would help me clear my head and think about what I wanted. And make me forget all about Felix freaking Jameson. I could charge my crystals and reverse whatever he did to me, too.

"Okay, I don't know why you're badgering me about this, but okay, I'll go," I finally said.

"Good, you need a vacation. You work too hard," Avery said with a smile.

I should have questioned that smile. I should have recognized my sister was up to something.

CHAPTER EIGHT

FELIX

I stood in the doorway of Skye's bedroom as she frantically packed for her trip down the shore with the Parks.

"That's why I told you to pack last night, half pint," I said.

"Don't rub it in!" she shrieked as she ran around her room.

"You want help?"

"No!"

I shook my head at her, but the doorbell ringing downstairs distracted me.

Skye gave me a panicked look. "I'm not ready."

"I'll get it."

I walked downstairs and opened the door to find Christine Park and her daughter Sophia behind it. Christine was in her mid-thirties. She had the same tawny brown skin as her brother Ryan and kind, dark eyes. Sophia looked like her spitting image.

"Come in," I said to them. "Skye's still getting her stuff together."

Sophia bounded up the steps without a word, and I shook my head.

Christine shrugged. "Teenagers. How are you doing, Felix?"

I ran a hand down my face. "Tired. You want coffee or something?"

She shook her head. "I'll stop at Wawa on the way. You look like you could really use that vacation."

I nodded and sat on the couch.

Once Skye left, I'd start my long drive to the Poconos. It might sound lonely, but I was looking forward to being alone with my thoughts for the week.

"Thanks for taking her this week."

Christine squeezed my arm. "Any time. Skye's a joy to have. I know that's all you."

I nodded.

"Fe, you've done an amazing job. Being a single parent isn't easy, but we're here for you and Skye."

"I know, Chris. You've helped me more than you know."

She smiled at me. "You're a good dad. You'll be amazing when you have your own kids."

I grimaced. Yeah, no. I loved my sister, but raising kids was hard. I never expected I would end up raising my sister because my dad lost himself in drugs. When I told people I didn't want kids, they acted like I was a monster.

Christine checked her watch. "Girls! Let's get a move on!" she yelled up the stairs.

It sounded like elephants were clomping down the steps instead of two teenage girls.

"Half pint, be good for the Parks, okay?"

My sister gave me a hug. "I'll be fine! Enjoy your vacation. You deserve it, big bro."

Christine smiled at me, and she ushered the two girls out of the house. They ran to the car together, where Christine's husband was sitting in the driver's seat waiting.

I ran a hand through my hair as I stood in the open front door. "Reception might be spotty, but call or email me if something comes up."

She gave me a smile. "Fe, stop being such a helicopter parent."

"She's my entire world."

Christine nodded in understanding. "I get it. Sophia's my whole world, but you still need a life. Have fun fishing in the Poconos."

I laughed. "Hiking. I don't even know how to fish."

"What?" she laughed. "Then why bother going up there?"

I shrugged. "Because Avery MacGregor offered, and I don't have to pay for a hotel. And I need a vacation."

"Skye will be fine without you. She's a teenage girl. She doesn't need you being a monk."

Hmm. This sounded familiar. I wondered if Skye had been echoing Christine's words to me.

"Maybe you can get laid at least. It seems like you need it."

"Christine!"

She gave me a mischievous grin. "What? Have a vacation fling. It could be fun!"

Maybe a vacation fling would help me get Gemma Jensen out of my head. My dick didn't seem to want to picture anyone else when I jacked off in the shower. I really couldn't go there, but my horny brain didn't want to let go of her. The stubborn woman was haunting me.

"Have fun!" Christine called back to me as she walked down the steps of my porch and into her car.

I stood on the porch waving to my sister and waited until the car had sped away, then I went back inside. Unlike Skye, I packed up my stuff yesterday. I had to load up the car, then I could leave.

I went upstairs for my suitcase and brought it out to the car. I had half a case of Radle My Cage and another half of Mac Daddy, perfect for a week at the cabin. I took the beer and my cooler packed with food out to the car next. I'd make a trip to the local grocery store on my way to the cabin for any last-minute supplies.

I got the car packed and locked up the house before I left. The Jensen's cabin was a two and half hour drive, but for once in my life, I was planning to enjoy the peace and quiet.

Three long hours later, I made it. It was much bigger than I had pictured. I imagined a tiny hunting cabin in the middle of nowhere, but I found a two-story log cabin in the woods that looked out onto an enormous lake. It perfectly combined a lake and forest backdrop. I dug it. I liked it better than the rental cabins I saw on the drive in. Avery had mentioned it was a tourist area, but I didn't mind that. Especially when I felt secluded back here.

I parked my car in front of the detached garage and got out. I lugged my beer up the steps of the big wraparound porch, pulled the key Avery had given me out of my back pocket, and keyed inside. The cabin's interior looked exactly how I imagined. It had wood paneling throughout but an upgraded kitchen with granite countertops and new-looking appliances. There was an enormous fireplace in the living room, but with the summer's heat, I probably wouldn't use it. Avery and Nolan must have enjoyed it when they honeymooned up here.

I put my beer into the fridge and started unloading my food. After bringing in all the cold stuff, I retrieved my suitcase and art supplies. I climbed the stairs and discovered there were three bedrooms. I picked the biggest one with the en suite bathroom, dropped my bags on the floor, and flopped down on the bed with a sigh.

It was weird to have zero responsibilities. I kinda wanted to lie in this bed and sleep for a thousand years.

I pulled out my phone and smiled when I saw my sister texted a picture of her and Sophia at the beach. I had to admit; it was nice that I didn't have to worry about her this week. Christine and her husband would take care of Skye like they always had. She was safe, and I could enjoy this week alone.

Tonight, I'd have a chill night since I was beat after the long drive in. Tomorrow, I'd get up and explore. Maybe I'd take the kayak Avery mentioned was in the garage out for a relaxing day on the water. I wanted to check out the trails and the nature preserve, too. I could take some photos and start a new painting. With my graphic design work, I hadn't been doing much painting. I sketched a lot, but I hadn't had time for my first love.

I set my phone down on the bedside table, walked back downstairs into the kitchen, and grabbed a bottle of Radle My Cage from out of the fridge. I popped the top with the beer opener magnet I found on the fridge. I laughed when I noticed it was a MacGregor Brothers Brewing Company one. Because, of course, it was. I squinted at the logo in thought. I wanted to tweak it, but I'd talk to Declan about that after vacation. The logo was one of the first things I designed. The typeface looked dated now, and I wanted to give it a refresh. The kerning was off, too.

I sipped on my beer while surveying the photos pinned to the fridge. There was one of Avery and Nolan cozy on the couch. He had his big hands on her pregnant belly, and the love between them poured out of the photo. I spied Gemma in a couple other photos that spanned the years. It was weird seeing her with her natural dark brown hair. I saw the resemblance between her and Avery in the older photos. The bright pink in your face color suited Gemma much better. I stared at a photo of a woman who looked like Avery's spitting image holding a toddler that was probably Gemma.

A sadness hit my chest that losing our moms was something we had in common. At least her mother hadn't wanted to go. In the photo, you could tell the woman loved her child. I thought my mom loved me, but then she left us to fend for ourselves.

Since Mom left, all I had done was care for my sister. I'd let partners down because Skye was more important to me. It wasn't until after Roger and I broke up that I realized trying to have it all wasn't possible. I couldn't hold down two jobs, parent Skye, and have a committed relationship. I had to choose. So I chose work and my sister. I didn't regret my decision, but sometimes the loneliness was unbearable. It didn't matter how I felt, though, because Skye was more important than anything.

I tried not to think about it and took another swig of my beer. I fired up the grill on the porch and made steaks for me, myself, and I. I was taking advantage of this solo vacation and going to enjoy every minute.

CHAPTER NINE

GEMMA

I forgot it was a long drive up to the cabin, but as I got closer, I got excited about my vacation. Was I annoyed that my sister sided with my boss? Yes. But maybe Declan and Avery were right that I needed a break.

I might not be working at the brewery this week, but I already scheduled a bunch of posts for our socials because I didn't trust Declan to know what he was doing. He might ask April to do it again, but she didn't even use hashtags. Avery said I should log out of the accounts or delete the apps from my phone so I wasn't tempted to do work, but I was afraid no one else would post stuff correctly.

Shit.

No wonder Declan wanted me to be his marketing director. I was already acting like it, and we both knew it. I just didn't want the pressure of it. Anxiety swelled in my chest at the idea of letting Declan down if I took the job and failed spectacularly.

I tried hard not to think about work as I drove my car up

the driveway. I looked up at the log cabin and sighed a breath of relief. I loved our little secluded cabin in the woods.

I spent many summers here with Dad after Mom died. After Avery went to college, she never had any interest in spending her summers off at the cabin. So it was just me and Dad. He taught me to fish, and I spent my summers kayaking and swimming in the lake. And kissing a lot of boys *and* girls. It took me a while to figure out I was bisexual. I told Dad during a fishing trip while we were on the boat. I was afraid of his reaction, especially since men his age didn't 'get' bisexuality. Dad had laughed and said, "I know." Good ole dad!

I was gonna take advantage of a week away from Drakesville. I planned to hike, fish, and be one with nature. I brought my jewelry making kit too, so I could make new items to put in my online shop. I didn't make any real money off my crystal jewelry; I did it for fun. I had a couple of repeat customers, but mostly it was my friends and family.

I cut the engine and got out of my car. I got the important stuff out first—my beer. I had a half case of 611 Ale and another of Area 267, two of my favorite beers the brewery made. I loved the artwork Felix did for both of them. They were very Pennsylvanian and screamed Drakesville.

Ugh, Felix!

I didn't want to think about him right now. I should have a fling this week and get him off my mind. I'd have to meet someone in person because the internet was spotty here. Not like I was having much luck on the apps lately, anyway.

I got out of my car and carried my beer into the cabin. When I opened the fridge, I was surprised to find a lot of

MacGregor Brothers beer already in there. That was odd. Normally, I'd assume it was leftover from Dad and Uncle Bill's last fishing trip, but there was an entire case in the fridge. I set my beer down on the table and noticed some of the beer was Mac Daddy. I didn't know if Mac Daddy was available in stores yet. We just released it at the brewery. A suspicious tingle went down my spine.

I checked the shared family calendar on my phone, just in case Avery was mistaken about no one using the cabin this week, but I was the only one on the list. Unless Dad made an impromptu trip, but he hadn't said anything when I went to get my fishing poles from his house this morning. Maybe my cousin Mason came up and forgot to clear it with Dad? That was okay. There was room for both of us. Although, Mason's taste in beer leaned toward IPAs like mine, and he hated the Radler. He said it tasted like a hard lemonade.

Odd. Maybe he brought a new girlfriend with him.

I brought the rest of my stuff in and tried to forget about the mystery beer. I put my things into the smaller bedroom I usually stayed in. If Mason was here, he probably took the primary bedroom. I put my stuff away and started to plan my vacation. If I wanted to fish today, I had to go buy bait. But I was in the mood for a hike at the nature preserve instead. I could go fishing tomorrow. I'd get breakfast in town at the coffee shop and grab bait at the tackle shop next door.

"Okay, hike today, and then maybe dinner at The Lakeside Bar. Tomorrow I can do my fishing and kayaking," I said out loud to myself.

I left the cabin and drove over to the nature preserve. I breathed in the fresh air as I got out of my car and started my hike. With the sun kissing my skin as I walked, I knew it would be a good week. The universe was putting out good vibes today, and I knew I'd figure out my career after this week. Mother nature would help me.

☀

Hiking alone wasn't the smartest idea, but I knew these woods like the back of my hand. After trekking through the forest, I was wiped and needed a drink.

I definitely didn't feel like cooking tonight after hiking and the long drive up, so I drove over to The Lakeside Bar on the resort side of the lake. The resort had several inn-style houses with guest rooms, rental cottages, and a couple of big houses for temporary stays. It was nice, but I preferred my dad's cabin in the woods. The bar was on the main dock with an amazing view of the expansive lake.

I parked it at the bar and took off my hat. I ran my fingers through my hair and put my hat back on. I could use a shower, but I needed to eat first. I peered over at the draft taps and was disappointed I didn't see any MacGregor Brothers beer. I'd talk to Declan about branching out sales in this part of the state.

And...I was thinking about work again.

Goddamnit.

Declan had a point about the marketing director thing. I was supposed to be on vacation, but all my thoughts were consumed by marketing ideas and sales pitches for the brewery. But the fear of failure was too great for me to consider his offer.

"Gemma!" a familiar voice called to me cheerily.

At the other end of the bar, a portly, grey-haired man stood behind the register. Ron had been managing The Lakeside Bar my entire life.

"Hey, Ron!" I said.

"I'll be right with ya!"

I waved him off and perused the menu. I didn't need to look because I already knew the menu by heart. One of the beers on tap was local, so I wanted to try that. I liked trying different beers and reporting back to Nolan. It felt like I was a spy. A beer spy.

Ron walked over to me and gave me a big smile. "Gemma, how are you?"

"Good. You still working here?" I asked.

He laughed. "Still here. Your dad in town?"

I shook my head. "Just me."

"Just you? That sister of yours not with you?"

"Nope! Avery just had a baby. I'm kinda on a forced vacation," I admitted with a grimace.

"Let me put your order in. Then you can tell me about that last part."

"Can I get the local IPA and the crab cakes?"

"You got it!"

I leaned back in my chair and waited for him to put my order in. He came back a couple minutes later and handed me the beer.

I took a sip and felt myself get blasted by hops. I liked a hoppy beer, but this was too much. Nolan's IPAs were so much better.

"So forced vacation? You in the doghouse?" Ron joked.

I laughed. "My boss wants me to accept a promotion, but I don't want it. He made me go on vacation to think about it."

"You still at the brewery?"

I nodded. "Yup. Oh, and my sister married the brewmaster."

"No, shit?"

I pulled out my phone and found a picture of Avery, Nolan, and the baby and showed it to him.

"Good for her. So what's the promotion?"

"Nolan's younger brother does the business side, sales and marketing, and he wants me to become the marketing director."

"That's good, right?"

I sighed. "Too much pressure! I love being a bartender."

Ron nodded. "I understand that. You'll figure it out."

I took a sip of my beer and thought about it. Everyone seemed so confident in my abilities, but I wasn't so sure.

I drank my beer while I waited for my food and tried to enjoy the atmosphere. Families were pouring in for the dinner rush while I sat at the bar thinking about my life. When Ron brought my crab cakes, I ate them like an animal. I had been pretty hungry.

I didn't want to stick around at the bar since I needed to shower away the dirt and grime from my hike. I could tell the guy beside me was eyeing me up, but I wasn't interested. He was too preppy and clean-cut. Not my type. I finished my beer and left Ron a hefty tip before heading out.

I drove back to the cabin in good spirits, but I felt them drop when I pulled up into the driveway and saw an unfamiliar car. I parked next to it in confusion. Maybe Mason *was* here. Did he get a new car? It had PA plates, so it had to be someone we knew. Unless a renter got lost looking for their cabin.

I felt unease spread through me as I got out of my car and went inside. I heard the shower on upstairs, and it sounded like it was coming from the attached bath in the primary bedroom. Was it Mason? Dad? Uncle Bill? It would explain the case of beer in the fridge. Why didn't Dad say anything when I got my fishing poles?

A sketchbook on the kitchen table caught my eye, and that struck me as odd. No one in my family was artistic except for me. Nobody else was on the family calendar, but it was clear I wasn't alone at the cabin.

I cautiously walked up the steps and checked the third bedroom, but there was no sign of anyone else. I gingerly opened the door to the primary bedroom. A suitcase was open on the bed, and a pile of dirty clothes was on the floor, but that didn't tell me anything. I walked into the room and searched for clues. On the bedside table, a watch caught my eye. It looked familiar to me, but my mind was blank.

Who was at the cabin with me?

I jumped at the sound of the bathroom door opening, and someone walked out. My breath caught in my throat as Felix Jameson walked into the bedroom wearing nothing but a towel.

Felix!

Fucking Felix was at my dad's cabin.

"What the fuck?" I screamed out loud.

My outburst startled Felix, who dropped his towel and looked up at me in alarm. I couldn't control myself as my eyes tracked down his glistening, wet body. I studied the tattoos down his arms until my eyes landed on his dick. Of course, my horny brain locked onto that.

We stared at each other in shock for several seconds until Felix registered who I was. "Gemma?"

I groaned.

Why was Felix Jameson naked and in my dad's cabin? And why did I get the feeling Avery set us up? I was gonna kill my sister.

CHAPTER TEN

FELIX

*I*t took me way longer than it should have to realize Gemma had caught me with my pants down. Or rather my towel. Avery assured me no one would be here this week. So why the fuck was her sister standing in front of me pretending she wasn't staring at my dick like she wanted to choke on it again?

What the fuck?

"AVERY!" we growled out in unison.

Gemma turned away from me. I shrugged it off, shoved on a pair of boxers and jeans, and searched for a t-shirt.

"You can turn around," I said with a laugh. "Who knew Gemma Jensen was so modest?"

"I'm not."

I pulled my t-shirt over my head. "What? You can't handle seeing me naked? Does it make you want to get on your knees and suck my cock again?"

Her eyes flashed with anger, and she threw a pillow at

my head. I ducked just in time for her to miss. "You're such an asshole!"

I gave her a sly grin. "Aw, you know you don't mean that, sweet thing."

She curled her hands into fists. "Why are you at my dad's cabin?"

"I could ask you the same thing."

"It's my dad's cabin," she said with a hard look that could have melted a lesser man.

I rubbed a hand through my beard. "Right, but your sister said I could stay up here this week. Why are you here?"

"Forced vacation," she muttered under her breath.

I didn't know what that meant, and she didn't elaborate. The pink-haired woman in front of me looked like a ball of rage. Her chest heaved and she clenched her jaw. So much for getting her to forget about me.

"I'm going home," she huffed out, and she started to storm out of the room, but I spun her around and grabbed her arm.

"Wait, a second. It's already dark, and it's a long way home. How about we call a truce?"

"What?" she spat out.

"How about...we share the cabin for the week? I do my thing, and you do yours. I promise I won't get in your way. At least stay the night. It's late."

"No. Fuck you!" she screeched. "Ugh, I can't believe you're here."

"Gem."

She pointed a finger at me. "No. I was supposed to take this week to be alone with my thoughts. You weren't supposed to be here."

"Okay, but how about we act like adults? I'm not asking you to share a bed with me."

"FINE!" she yelled and stormed off down the hall. I cringed at the sound of a door slamming behind her. So much for some peace and quiet this week.

One thing was for sure: Avery definitely set us up.

I pulled out my phone and shot off a text to the other Jensen sister.

ME: *Umm, care to explain yourself?*

Avery mentioned cell service could be spotty, but so far, my texts had been coming in okay. My phone buzzed with a reply.

AVERY: [*Angel emoji*]

I rubbed a frustrated hand across my face and typed back.

ME: *AVS! Your sister's here.*

AVERY: *You need to work out your differences. And tell her WHY you're a dick to her. Gem will understand.*

ME: *You know?*

AVERY: *Of course. Nol told me.*

I honestly hadn't expected that. Nolan was the kind of guy who kept shit close to the vest, but Avery was his wife, and he worshiped the ground she walked on. Who was I kidding? Of course, he told his wife.

ME: *Why are you doing this?*

AVERY: *Payback. Gemma pushed me toward Nol, and now it's your turn.*

I groaned and dropped my phone on the bed.

Fucking Avery. I didn't realize she could be so meddlesome. I half wondered if she and Declan planned this together because Declan had agreed to give me time off a little too quickly. He had a weird look in his eye when I told him Avery offered to let me stay at the cabin.

ME: *Did you concoct this plan with Dec?*

AVERY: *I plead the fifth.*

Assholes. Meddling assholes, the both of them.

With a sigh, I got off the bed and went downstairs to make something quick for dinner. Gemma hadn't come downstairs when I finished cooking my pasta, and that was fine with me. It was better if we stayed out of each other's way this week. Although, I was sure I'd wake up tomorrow, and she'd be gone. I was fine with that, too.

I took my dinner outside and sat on the porch with my sketchbook while I ate and sketched the landscape. I had to admit; it was beautiful up here. I planned to go back to the nature preserve tomorrow with my sketchbook. I was considering taking my canvas and paints, too.

A bottle of Mac Daddy appeared in my view, and I looked up and saw Gemma holding out the beer to me. She held a bottle of Area 267 in her other hand, and she looked uncomfortable.

I cocked my head at her.

"Okay, truce?" she asked and waved the beer at me.

I took the beer from her and sipped on it silently. I loved a good hefeweizen, but a lot of people didn't know the difference between an American wheat and a hefeweizen. Not Nolan, though. He got it right with the distinct banana and clove flavor, and I loved it.

Gemma walked down to the fire pit while I drank my beer on the porch. She had changed into jeans and a hoodie, and had pulled her bright hair into a messy bun on top of her head. The change in clothes was likely because of the chill in the night air. I watched her collecting wood and putting it into the fire pit. At one point, she walked over to the garage and got an ax out. I watched as her lithe figure started splitting logs like a mountain woman and tossing them into the pit. I never guessed she was so outdoorsy.

"Hey, maybe I should have drawn you as the lumberjack on this beer!" I called down to her.

That got me a middle finger, and I snickered to myself.

Gemma disappeared from view and then came back and lit the fire. She walked back up the steps and went inside. When she came back out, she handed me a stick and was holding a bag of marshmallows.

"It's not the first night of vacation if I don't have a fire," she explained.

She didn't wait for me to follow her. I closed my sketchbook and put it back inside. I took my beer and stick and walked down to join her. She was already roasting her marshmallow while she sipped on her gross hoppy beer in front of the fire.

I sat in the camping chair next to her, stuck a marshmallow onto my stick, and put it into the fire. She turned her stick and pulled it out, coming back with a barely toasted marshmallow. She closed her eyes as she took it off her stick and popped it into her mouth.

"I love the first fire of summer," she said with a dreamy sigh.

"I didn't know you were so outdoorsy," I mused while pulling my stick out of the fire. My marshmallow was nice and crispy. If I had left it in much longer, it would have been charred and black.

"Ew! That's burnt. It's so gross!" she said and pretended to puke.

I smiled at her as I popped it into my mouth. "Just the way I like it."

We sat in silence for a couple of minutes. I sipped on my beer and watched as she closed her eyes. The wind blew stray hair in her face, and I couldn't help but notice how at peace she looked.

"I still fucking hate you," she said, and those gorgeous blue eyes of hers popped open. She glared when she noticed I was staring.

I sipped my beer and didn't say anything. She had every right to hate me. I deserved it after I treated her like garbage and made her feel like she was worthless. I deserved every hateful glare and snappy retort she sent my way.

She stared into the fire. "If you stay out of my way, I'll stay out of yours. The cabin's big enough for both of us. I wish Avery hadn't meddled, but I'm not going anywhere."

"Okay, works for me."

She eyed me suspiciously while she drank her beer, then set it down and took a picture of it with her phone. I didn't think anything of it because Gemma was always taking weird pictures to post on the brewery's social media accounts.

Wait. What had she meant about a forced vacation?

"What did you mean earlier?" I asked.

"When?"

"About a 'forced vacation.' What does that mean?"

"Nothing," she snapped.

I held up my hands and drank my beer in silence beside her. I watched her profile as she leaned back against the chair. The light of the fire reflected off the colors in her hair, and she looked so beautiful. It made me want to sketch her, but she'd stab me with her stick if I did that.

We sat quietly in front of the fire together, drinking our beers and eating too many marshmallows. We barely spoke, both of us too tired for yet another screaming match. I could tell something was bothering her, but I wasn't going to poke the bear. I had already annoyed her enough by my mere existence.

After I downed a second beer, the fire started to go out. I was exhausted from my day at the nature preserve and ready for bed. "You need help putting out the fire?" I asked.

"I got it," she said with a hint of indignation.

"You sure, sweet thing?" I teased.

"Oh, my god! Fuck off into the sun, Felix! I know what I'm doing."

Gemma hated being called 'sweet thing,' and I only called her that to annoy her. I said it once during a bitter argument, and then never stopped in an effort to keep up my asshole appearance. But honestly? It was fitting. Gemma was a sweet thing to everyone else but me. The regulars loved her, and everyone who worked at the brewery listened to her whenever she had a new marketing plan. When she roped everyone into helping with her sister's wedding at the brewery, no one said no. Because how could you say no when Gemma gave you that pretty smile and those big blue puppy dog eyes? You couldn't.

I smiled at her and took her empty beer bottles with me inside. This week was going to be interesting. I watched Gemma from the window for a few seconds before climbing the steps to my room. I shut the door behind me and undressed for bed.

I thought I would fall asleep as soon as my head hit the pillow, but of course, my horny brain had other thoughts. Every time I closed my eyes, memories of my night with Gemma flashed before them.

"Fuck," I swore as I reached a hand down and gripped my enraged dick.

I slid my hand up and down my shaft as I remembered the sounds of Gemma's moans. Images of that night assaulted my brain as I stroked myself harder. It didn't take long before I shot my load onto my stomach.

As I cleaned myself off in the bathroom, the reality of the situation sunk in. I was so totally fucked. There was no way Gemma and I could survive this week without wanting to kill each other. Or worse. But crawling into bed together again was a terrible idea.

CHAPTER ELEVEN

GEMMA

I got up early and left before Felix woke up. I thought about driving back to Drakesville, but then I thought, 'fuck that, I'm going to enjoy this vacation.' If we stayed out of each other's way, I could manage. Besides, I'd be staying far away from Felix today by spending the day on the water fishing. But first I needed some supplies.

I drove into town and went to the local coffee shop for breakfast. The blonde woman behind the counter looked vaguely familiar, but I couldn't quite place her.

Her eyes lit up in recognition when she saw me. "Oh my god, Gemma!"

I furrowed my brow until I realized it was Harper.

Harper and I had spent a couple of weeks exploring our sexuality when I was fifteen. She was bi-curious, whereas kissing her made me realize a lot about myself. When I kissed her all those years ago, I'd admit, it confused me. Especially when I kissed a boy the next day. Then my brain went, 'ooohh.' I hadn't seen Harper in a couple of years, but I knew she still lived in town.

"Hey, Harp. How are you?" I asked.

"Great. I didn't know you were in town. I haven't seen your dad yet."

I shook my head. "Just me this time."

"Well, it's great to see you. What can I get you?"

"Bacon, egg, and cheese on an everything bagel and a caramel macchiato."

She gave me a bright smile, the kind I used to long for when I was a teenager. Harper was my past, but it was nice we had no hard feelings. I knew better than anyone that figuring out your sexuality could be a challenge.

I sat at a table in the back and waited for my order. Wi-Fi and cell reception were better in town, so I called my sister.

I didn't even let her say hello. "You suck, you know that, right?"

Avery laughed on the other line. "You pushed me toward Nolan. I'm returning the favor."

I groaned. "Avs, I HATE him."

"Do you really?"

No. Not really. I wanted to. I wanted to hate him for being an asshole, but I couldn't. I couldn't stop thinking about him. I even touched myself to the idea of fucking him again last night. It was another reason I left so early this morning and planned to take the boat out fishing all day. I couldn't look him in the eye, knowing I did that. But good god, he was so hot. With his tattoos and that mischievous smile and the way he practically purred out 'sweet thing' to me. I had to keep my distance this week, or I was going to do something reckless, like sleep with him again.

I wouldn't tell my sister the truth, though. That I only

pretended to hate the hot tattooed and pierced bartender because if I didn't, I'd have to admit how much he hurt me. I shouldn't have been so crushed by being stood up. Yeah, it sucked, but it shouldn't have shattered my heart the way it did. And when I slept with him, I knew it didn't mean anything, but my heart still ached when I woke up alone.

"We don't need to work out our differences. He's an asshole, end of story," I said into my phone instead. Harper brought over my order, and I waved thanks at her as I sipped my coffee.

"So...you're on your way home, then?" Avery asked.

"No," I grumbled. "We agreed to a truce. He stays out of my way; I stay out of his."

"Okay..." Avery trailed off, but in a tone that meant she didn't believe me. "What are you up to today, then?"

"Gonna take the boat out and fish."

"Is that safe by yourself?"

I scoffed. I had been taking the boat out with my dad since I was fourteen. I knew what I was doing. I was eccentric and flighty, but I hated that she treated me like her practice kid.

"Yes, Mom!"

"Shut up, you brat! You're my sister, and I love you. Have fun this week!"

"I don't enjoy being tricked into a vacation, Avs."

"It was for your own good."

My own good, my ass.

"You should take the job," she said.

I groaned. "Avs, please."

"You're good at this, Gem. Declan wouldn't pressure you to take the job if he didn't think you were capable. I know you love being a bartender, but the marketing director job would look great on your resume."

"But I love working at the brewery."

She sighed. "You might change your mind one day and want to move on. Being the marketing director would open doors for you."

"Did you forget how you had to pull me out of bed after my mental breakdown?"

I could almost see her pursing her lips in thought. "This will be different. Declan believes in you. It's time you believe in yourself, too."

"Yeah, yeah, yeah," I grumbled, and changed the subject to asking her about the baby. That at least got her distracted enough to stop pestering about my career crisis.

We talked for a while longer until I hung up because my breakfast was getting cold. I finished my coffee and food and grabbed a to-go sandwich and snacks for my lunch on the boat.

"It was good to see you, Gem," Harper said as she rang me up.

"You too."

"Hey, how long are you in town for?"

"Probably a week. Why?"

"Let's grab a drink sometime."

"Sure! But don't get mad if I'm a beer snob."

She laughed. "That's right, your dad said you work for a brewery."

"Yup. I'll see you later. The fish aren't gonna catch themselves."

I walked over to the bait and tackle shop to pick up minnows, then drove to the marina where we docked the boat. Fortunately, we docked our boat on the other side of the lake, so there was no chance of running into Felix. For once, I was glad about the inconvenience. I dropped my supplies inside the boat and started her up. Our boat wasn't enormous, it fit a few people comfortably, but it was perfect for a solo fishing session.

I drove the boat out onto the lake, where I knew I could catch trout or striped bass. I was wearing my bikini under my clothes, so I took my shirt off. I put my hat on my head and slathered up my pale body with sunblock. Working so much at the brewery, I didn't get outdoors like I wanted. On my days off, I slept in and did errands instead of going out and exploring the local parks in our area. There was a lake in Bucks County I hadn't explored since I moved back to the 'burbs. I'd have to remedy that when I got home.

It was a perfect summer day for fishing. If I caught something good today, I could make a fish fry for dinner. The sun shone down on my skin, and I felt good vibes radiating from the earth. So what if I had to share the cabin with Felix? That was okay. I could deal. He'd do whatever he wanted, and I'd enjoy my time solo fishing or hiking. This would be totally fine.

I put my bait on my hook and cast out my line. Fishing might bore some, but for me, it reminded me of time spent with my dad. We had the most intimate conversations out on the boat together. I wouldn't have come out to him if we hadn't been out fishing. Dad wouldn't have told me he didn't want to date because nobody compared to my mom if we hadn't been on the boat. Avery didn't know that because Dad asked me not to tell her. She worried about him too much already.

I rubbed my rose quartz necklace as I thought about my mom. I lived more of my life without her than with her. I wracked my brain for memories of her, but they were fuzzy. Most of my best childhood memories came from my single dad raising me and teaching me all the outdoorsy shit I loved. I liked fishing, hiking, and building the first fire of summer vacation, all because of my dad. My best memories were up here in the Poconos.

I frowned as the sad thoughts of my mother enveloped me. I didn't want to send morose thoughts out into the universe today. I took my crystals out of my pocket and let them charge underneath the summer sunlight while I closed my eyes and let the heat of the sun warm my skin.

As I sat in the boat waiting for the first bite on my line, my thoughts shifted to work. I thought about scheduling more posts for our social media channels and seeing what other community events we could get involved with. We missed out on the farmer's market this year, but we could apply next year. We already had the Arts Fest lined up for the fall again.

Shit, maybe I *should* be the marketing director for the brewery.

Something tugged at my line and pulled me out of my thoughts. I grabbed my fishing pole and lifted it up at a forty-five-degree angle. I waited for the drag to stop and lifted my pole up. I reeled in when I brought the pole back down in the fish's direction. I repeated the action until I had the fish in the boat.

"Yes!" I squealed in delight.

"What ya get?" another fisher called over to me.

"Brown trout!" I yelled back.

"Atta girl!"

Pride swelled in my chest at a job well done. I took care of the fish as quickly and humanely as possible before I put it in my pile and redid my line. I didn't enjoy hunting or fishing for sport. If mother earth gave me something useful, I didn't want to throw it away.

I spent the next few hours on the lake but didn't catch any more fish. I must have gotten lucky with that first one. I was sun-kissed and in high spirits when I drove the boat back to the dock.

But my spirits deflated when I got back to the cabin and saw Felix's car in the drive. I took a quick shower and started preparing the fish for dinner. Killing your own dinner was cool, since you knew where it came from, but it was still kinda gross. I made filets and fried them up on the stove while I played my rockabilly playlist and drank a beer.

I hadn't even noticed Felix until I turned around and saw him leaning against the fridge, beer in hand. He watched me with hungry eyes, and I didn't like that. He was so hot, but we would never, ever sleep together again.

"What are you making?" he asked.

"Fish fry. I caught it myself!"

He raised his pierced eyebrow, and something about the gesture made me want to yank it out. That was a mean thought, but I was still pissed off at him. I would try to play nice this week since we were in such close quarters, but a part of me didn't want to. I kinda wanted to punch him and then suck his dick.

Jesus H, what was wrong with me?

"I didn't know you fished. Is that safe to eat?" he asked.

I shrugged. "As long as you don't eat it all the time. There's enough for both of us. If you want to join me for dinner."

Why was I inviting him to have dinner with me?

He smirked. "Sure, sweet thing."

"Gah!" I said and glared at him. "Never mind, you're the literal worst."

"Relax. You need help?"

"Oh yeah, there's a bag of fries in the freezer. We'll bake them in the oven and have fish and chips."

"I'm game."

He helped me get everything ready for dinner, which was nice. He knew his way around a kitchen, and that interested me. It shouldn't have. I really should not care about Felix's culinary skills.

We ate in silence. The trout was good fried up, but I think it tasted better since I caught it myself. Felix didn't let me get up after dinner while he did the dishes. I sat back and drank my beer. Then I got up and started taking photos of my beer in different spots in the house.

"Are you doing work?" Felix asked when he found me outside on the porch.

I grimaced. "Yeah."

He took my phone out of my hands. "Vacation, Gemma. It means no working."

"I can't help it!" I said and grabbed for my phone.

"No work."

When I nodded, he handed it back, but I was a liar.

"It's beautiful here," Felix said.

I looked at his profile while he stared out at the horizon. There was something haunting in his dark eyes, a secret hidden there. Part of me wanted to know his secrets, but the other part was still raw. I couldn't give him another chance to crush me into a thousand pieces.

I jumped at the sound of thunder in the distance as a strike of lightning lit up the sky.

"You okay?" he asked.

I nodded.

But I wasn't. I hated thunderstorms. And when the rain poured down suddenly, I ran inside without another word. Felix didn't stop me when I ran upstairs and hid in my room for the rest of the night. Thunderstorms like this reminded me of the day my mom died and made me feel awful because I barely remembered her.

Felix hadn't noticed I was being weird since I had already told him to stay out of my way this week. He must have assumed that was my way of being alone with my thoughts. That was true, but they weren't particularly good thoughts. Instead, I sat up in bed with my knees against my chest and let the guilt about my mom come to the surface.

CHAPTER TWELVE

FELIX

I lay in bed, listening to the rain pounding against the cabin. Gemma ran up to her room when it started pouring and hadn't come out. When that flash of lightning lit up the sky, a pained look crossed her face, and she darted inside as if something had spooked her.

It confused me because she had been in a good mood when I found her cooking dinner. She looked so proud when she told me about catching the fish. It was kinda cute. I had no idea she was so outdoorsy. I kinda dug it, though I shouldn't have.

I sketched as I listened to the rain and realized I was drawing Gemma. I drew the way her nose wrinkled when she was thinking too hard and how her eyes lit up when she got excited. I drew her pouty, full lips, remembering how good they felt on mine.

I was in over my head. Especially since the woman in question might murder me and bury me in these woods.

I peered up at the ceiling when the lights flickered a

couple of times. Then they went out entirely, engulfing me in darkness. I darted up in bed at the sound of a piercing scream. I was in dad mode, and it took me a second to realize it was Gemma and not my sister screaming. I set my sketchbook down on the bed and waited for the lights to come back on. After enduring a couple of minutes of darkness, I walked down the hall and knocked on Gemma's closed door.

"Gem? You okay?" I asked.

"Yes," she answered in a quiet voice.

Alarm coursed through me. She didn't sound okay.

"You screamed. Are you sure you're okay?" I asked.

"No."

"Can I come in?"

I strained to hear her response, but she squeaked out a meek yes. I opened the door and saw Gemma sitting up against the headboard of the bed with her arms wrapped around her knees. She looked so vulnerable. It was so uncharacteristic that alarm bells rang inside my head.

I fumbled around in the dark until I reached the bed and sat down on it. "What's wrong?"

My eyes had adjusted to the dark, and I saw her shake her head.

"You want me to leave you alone?" I asked.

She shook her head again and grabbed my hand. "Stay. Please?"

I couldn't refuse when she begged like that. I slid into the bed beside her and wrapped my arms around her. I didn't know what was wrong, but her entire demeanor had changed as soon as the storm started.

I stroked her hair as she leaned into my chest.

"I don't like thunderstorms," she blurted out after a few moments of silence had passed.

I stroked her hair, trying to soothe whatever was bothering her. I definitely shouldn't be lying in this bed, stroking her hair and holding her in my arms. It was only going to give my dick ideas.

"There's nothing to be afraid of. I'm sure the lights will come back on soon," I reassured her.

"I'm not afraid of the dark."

"Then what is it?"

"There was a thunderstorm when my mom died," she admitted in a small voice.

Oh.

"Sometimes, I don't remember her at all, and I feel guilty about that. Avery gets sad at Christmas because she misses Mom, but my memories are few and far between."

"You were young."

"When it pours like this, I remember being that scared little girl. I hate thunderstorms. It reminds me of the day my dad fell apart."

"Oh, Gem." I sighed.

I didn't know why I did it, but I leaned down and gently brushed my lips against hers. She didn't fight me. Instead, she mewed as I deepened the kiss. It was as if she had wanted me to kiss her. I framed her face with my hands and kissed her like a man starved. I kissed her like I was about to devour her whole.

I didn't realize what I was doing until I had her on her back flat against the bed and I settled myself on top of her. I pulled back, but she wrapped her arms around me and laced her hands through my hair. She pulled me down to her and kissed me back.

I broke the kiss again and studied her face. "Sweet thing, we shouldn't do this."

"I know," she admitted. "I hate you."

I kissed my way down the column of her throat until I was at the swell of her breasts. I lifted my head up before I slid the strap of her tank top down and pulled the material down to reveal the rounded globe of her breast. I dipped my head down and took her breast in my mouth. I lapped my tongue around her nipple, and she arched her back in pleasure at the motion.

"Mmm, more," she whispered.

"We shouldn't," I said again, but I pulled the other strap of her tank down and repeated the action with her other breast. God, those breasts. I wanted to slide my dick between them until I came all over them.

"I need this, please, Felix?"

"Why?" I asked, kissing my way back up to her pretty face.

"Because...I need it."

"You sure?" I asked.

She nodded.

"Okay..." I trailed off when the realization hit me. "Fuck."

"What's wrong?"

"I don't have any condoms."

She chewed on her lip for a moment, then sat up and took off her shirt. She shimmied underneath me to slip off her tiny shorts, and she wasn't wearing anything underneath them. I looked up at the ceiling and thought of Bulldogs hockey stats, so I didn't blow my load.

"I have an implant, but can you pull out?" she asked.

I shook my head. "No. No way. I'm not having sex without a condom."

"Just pull out!"

"Gem, I don't want kids."

"Me neither. That's why I have an implant."

I sighed. My dick was a hard spike against my leg. I wanted to be buried deep inside her, but going bare was dangerous. Birth control could still fail.

She ran a hand across my beard. "Come on my tits. Don't you want that, baby?"

Fuuuuuck.

Yes, I did. I wanted to come all over her. Why was I trying to say no?

"Are you sure?" I asked again. "What about other stuff?"

"I've been tested recently. I'm good. You?"

I nodded. "Me too."

She pulled my shirt over my head. "Please, Felix, I just need the comfort of your body tonight."

I should have stopped, but she was laid out beneath me, begging for my dick. How could I say no to that? I got up from the bed and took off my jeans and boxers, too.

I pumped my dick while I watched her slide her hand down to touch her clit. Gemma was naked and touching herself because I was taking too long to give her my dick. How in the hell did my fantasies come to life?

I pounced on the bed and pinned her beneath me. I wrapped my hand around her throat as I kissed her. "That's my job," I growled.

She bucked against my hand like she was trying to get away. I dropped my hand away, afraid I scared her with my need to be rough, but then she brought my hand back up to her throat.

"Oh, you like getting choked, huh?" I asked, and my lips curled up into a wolfish grin.

She held her hand up, showing two fingers up like a peace sign. "This is my safe motion. If I want you to stop, I'll do this."

"Okay. Proceed?"

She nodded.

I slipped my other hand down and circled her clit with my middle finger. She arched her hips up against me.

"Promise to behave?" I asked in her ear.

She nodded. "Please, Felix?"

I rubbed her clit until she came apart at the seams. But I didn't stop there. I kissed my way down her body until I had her legs over my shoulders while I feasted on her. I breathed in her sweet scent and wrapped my lips around her clit. I didn't stop until she gripped my hair with two hands and shouted out my name.

My dick was weeping to be inside her, so I didn't give her a moment to catch her breath before getting up and sliding inside her. She moaned and wrapped her legs around me as we moved together as if we were one. With one hand, I held her leg high against my hip while the other wrapped around her throat. I should have known a woman who liked to get her ass slapped and her hair pulled also loved being choked.

I was so stupid for doing this. This was such a bad idea, but I didn't care when I was bare inside her sweet pussy.

"Gemma, I'm not gonna last," I admitted as the bed rocked against the wall with each snap of my hips.

She reached down and caressed her clit again. "S'okay, keep doing that. Right there. Fuck, I needed this so bad, Felix."

I wasn't gonna ask her why getting fucked by me comforted her. I knew she was gonna kick me out as soon as she realized what a mistake this was. When she remembered how much she hated me. I wasn't a good guy when it came to her. If I was, I wouldn't be balls deep inside her without a condom with my hand around her throat.

What the fuck am I doing?

But my dick told me to shut the fuck up and enjoy it instead.

I rolled my hips and rode her hard. I put a little more pressure on her neck. I looked into her eyes, checking to make sure that was okay. She nodded at my unasked question, and she took my choking like a little brat taking her punishment.

"You hate me, but not my dick, huh? You want to choke on it again?" I asked and released my grip on her neck, but I didn't remove my hand.

"I love your dick. But you can get fucked."

"Such a brat," I growled and squeezed her neck again. "You're gonna get it good."

"Give it to me. Come on my tits. I want you to paint me with your cum."

Holy fucking shit.

I squeezed my eyes shut and pulled out just in time. I frantically pumped my dick and did as she asked. I came in long hot squirts across her beautiful chest. Fuck, it was so hot seeing her spread eagle with my cum all over her gorgeous tits. Like I had marked her as mine.

She dipped her finger into a pool of cum on her chest and slid it into her mouth. I felt like I was going to come again as I watched her suck my cum off her finger. Fuck, this woman was hot as hell in bed.

"Sweet thing," I groaned out.

"Hmm?"

I boxed her head with my arms. "That was so fucking hot, but dangerous as hell."

She frowned. "I know."

"Let me get you something to clean you up," I said.

I went into the bathroom across the hall and grabbed a

washcloth. I ran warm water over it and brought it to her. It shouldn't have been erotic, watching her clean my cum off her naked body, but it was. She set the washcloth down on the bedside table and leaned back on the bed with a sigh.

I kissed her again as we lay side-by-side in the bed. I kissed her neck where my hands had been and pushed her hair out of her face. Aftercare was always important to me.

"Okay?" I asked.

She nodded. "Yes, but thanks for asking."

"I wasn't too rough?" I asked and continued to press small kisses against her skin.

She shook her head. "No, you knew exactly what you were doing. I trusted you."

The rain outside had finally stopped, but the power hadn't come back on. I lay on my back and pulled her across my chest. I tried to tell myself not to notice how she fit so perfectly in my arms.

"I needed to feel loved tonight," she whispered.

I sighed. "Gemma, I can't give you what you want."

"I know. I'm not stupid. I'm not gonna let you break my heart a third time."

I couldn't ask her what she meant because she fell asleep shortly after, with her head on my chest, like she belonged there. I ran my hands through her hair and thought about what she said. I never should've slept with Gemma, and I had done it twice already. No wonder she hated me. I was such a dick.

I woke to a freezing bedroom, but Gemma wasn't next to me anymore. The power must have come back on when we fell asleep. I scrubbed a hand over my face and smoothed down my beard.

We shouldn't have done that. I made the situation between us worse.

I couldn't give her what she wanted. I couldn't give her the time and attention she deserved. Gemma needed a partner who could dote on her. A partner that gave her the world, and that wasn't me.

I rolled out of bed and went downstairs to find Gemma in the kitchen, making coffee and breakfast.

"Last night shouldn't have happened," she said firmly when she heard my footsteps.

"I'm sorry."

She shook her head. "Don't be. I was sad and lonely, and I needed comfort, but it's not happening ever again. I still hate you."

"Gemma."

"Save it," she snapped. "We both knew it was a mistake, and it can't happen again. "

I nodded. "Okay, whatever you want. I—I'm sorry."

She shook her head. "It's okay. I practically begged you to fuck me. I was sad and missing my mom, and I needed you to fuck the sadness out of me."

I nodded and watched her sip her coffee. I didn't think she remembered saying I broke her heart.

"It won't happen again," I said.

She stared at me for a moment. "Okay, BYE!"

I wanted to laugh at that. No amount of orgasms made this woman's attitude towards me change. I guess I should have been happy about that. Gemma wanted a partner, but I couldn't give her that.

I didn't stay to have breakfast with her, sensing she needed me to get out of her face. I drove into town and went to the coffee shop. The cheery blonde barista already knew me by name and gave me a big smile when I walked in. I ordered a black coffee and a pastry and sat at the window, lost in thought.

I pulled out my phone and texted Ryan.

ME: *I fucked up.*

RY: *Did you fuck Gemma again already?*

I furrowed my brow.

RY: *The big guy told me about his wife's meddling.*

ME: *Yeah. But she just wants me for my dick. She still hates me.*

RY: *Then give her that dick, dude! Who gives a fuck?*

I should listen to my friend, but I already treated Gemma awful. I felt like such a dick. I didn't want my little sister to end up with someone like me. She didn't deserve someone who tossed her aside and broke her heart repeatedly. Gemma didn't deserve how I treated her.

It didn't explain why I stopped at the pharmacy for a box of condoms, though.

CHAPTER THIRTEEN

GEMMA

*a*s soon as I discovered Felix at the cabin, I should have left. I kept saying I hated him, kept telling him how much I didn't like him, but that didn't stop me from practically begging him for sex last night. Who does that? Maybe I got too much sun yesterday.

But I knew that wasn't true. The thunderstorm made me sad. It made me miss the mother I barely remembered, and I just wanted to be held. Then he had to kiss me. That soft, reassuring kiss broke me, and then I couldn't help my horny brain from craving his dick. It was a bad idea when I let him go bare inside me. I never did that. Ever.

"Gemma?" a voice pulled me out of my thoughts, and I realized I was standing on the main dock staring at my boat.

I turned around and saw Harper, with a line of worry creasing her forehead. Next to her was a tall Black woman sporting bouncy, natural curls. They wore bikini tops and shorts, like they were ready for a day on the lake, much like myself. I planned to take the boat out to relax on the water. Far away from Felix Jameson and his kissable lips.

"Huh?" I asked.

The crease of worry in Harper's brow deepened. "Are you okay?"

I frowned. "Not really."

"Okay, take us out on your boat and tell us about it," Harper said and clapped her hands.

The other woman rolled her eyes. "Harper, that's rude."

I laughed and got into the boat. "No, hop in. I'm Gemma, by the way."

"Keisha," the other woman introduced herself. "I'm Harper's wife."

I tried to not let my surprise come across my features. I thought for sure Harper was just bi-curious.

I started the boat's engine and drove us to the middle of the lake.

"So, what's up, Gem?" Harper asked. She and her wife smeared sunblock on their bodies while I parked the boat.

I sighed. "I keep on making bad decisions."

"With what?" Keisha asked.

"I slept with someone I shouldn't have."

"Summer fling! Who cares?" Harper said with a grin.

I sighed again. "Only, we work together, and he's an asshole. And...my sister told him he could stay at the cabin this week."

"Okay, explain everything," Keisha said, and Harper sat up in interest.

So I did. I told them the whole story. About Felix standing me up, and pretending he never asked me out. How he seduced his way into my bed and then left in the morning. And how I got scared during the thunderstorm last night and needed comfort.

That was the part that made me feel the worst. It had been a moment of weakness, where I wanted to feel something. My heart was getting big, silly ideas, but I remembered what he said. He couldn't give me the love I wanted. But I let him into my bed, and he wormed his way into my heart again.

Keisha tapped her finger against her lips. "Okay...but what if you had a summer fling with him?"

"What?" I asked and gave her a weird look.

"Yeah!" Harper agreed. "What happens in the Poconos stays in the Poconos."

Keisha laughed. "Babe, that's Vegas."

"Same difference!"

I shook my head and lay out on the boat, letting the sun shine down on me. I pulled my sunglasses down onto my eyes.

"That's a terrible idea," I said. "He already broke my heart."

"Then tell your heart it's none of its business and get laid on vacation!" Harper said with a playful grin.

I laughed. "You two are enablers."

"Is he hot?" Keisha asked.

"God, so hot. He has a vibrating tongue ring! And he has a nice trimmed beard and sleeve tattoos. I'm weak for tattoos."

"Yours are pretty," Keisha said.

I rubbed my hand down my tattooed arm. "Thanks. Getting a full sleeve's a bitch, but I love them."

"They suit you, Gem. And the pink hair, it looks so you," Harper said with a smile.

"Thanks," I said and fingered the quartz around my neck.

Keisha and Harper looked so cute together. Harper and

I had a falling out when we were teenagers, and she said she wasn't 'supposed' to like women.

"Gem, I need to apologize for when we were teens," Harper said.

I waved my hand at her. "I get it. Coming out's scary. I thought my dad would throw me off the boat."

"No way! Your dad adores you. Every time he comes to town, he can't stop talking about how proud he is of both you and your sister. Oh! Last time he was in town, he was beaming about becoming a grandfather. Show us the baby pictures!"

I laughed and grabbed my phone and found the pictures of baby Norah to show them. They fawned over the photos, and Aunt pride swelled in my chest. I was still annoyed with my sister for meddling between me and Felix, but I still loved her. And she kept sending me the cutest pictures of Norah, so I couldn't stay mad at her.

"Her husband's a total lumberjack!" Harper said with a laugh.

We all laughed together. "Oh my god, I know! He's such a grump except with her. It's so cute."

I took my phone back and saw a text message from Declan.

DEC: *Stop posting on social media. Enjoy your vacation!*

I ignored his message and put my phone away.

I sat up and pulled out the plastic container with all my crystals and jewelry-making supplies. I sat up on the floor of the boat while Harper and Keisha sunned themselves. I started wrapping wires around a piece of clear quartz as the girls told me the story of how they met.

"What's that?" Keisha asked and pointed to what I was doing.

"Oh! I make jewelry with healing crystals. This is quartz. It's the master healer."

"Oh, cool. I noticed the one you wear around your neck," Keisha said, looking genuinely interested. My sister usually rolled her eyes when I talked about this stuff.

"Oh, yeah, it's rose quartz. It's the love stone. It's supposed to help restore trust and harmony in relationships."

"Hmm."

Harper nudged her wife. "Babe, don't be all 'hmm.' That usually means she wants to tell you something you don't want to hear."

I cocked my head at her and put my necklace away. I started working on the moonstone earrings I wanted to give Avery. "Say what you gotta say. I don't mind if you're blunt."

"Well, maybe that's why you keep sleeping with this guy. The stone draws you to him."

I shook my head. "I think it's because he's hot, and I'm horny with a capital H."

They both laughed, and I shrugged because it was true.

I made a few more pieces while we sunbathed on the lake. I got bored sitting in calm water, and cruised them around the lake. With the wind in my hair, I felt energized and recharged. Like the sun had charged me up like it did my crystals.

After a couple of hours on the boat, I brought us back to shore, and we parted ways. I lugged my stuff to the car and then walked back down onto the sandy man-made lake. I picked seashells as I strolled down the shoreline. The lake here wasn't a typical beach, but some shells washed ashore, and I liked to collect them. Maybe I should start making jewelry with the shells in addition to my crystals.

I pocketed the shells and forced myself to stop procrastinating about going back to the cabin. I had to face Felix, eventually. When I got back to the cabin, I spied him out on the dock. He stood with his shirt off in front of a canvas with a paint palette in one hand. I wasn't expecting that.

I dropped my stuff inside and grabbed us two Mac Daddy beers. I loved my hoppy IPAs, but Nolan did an awesome job with the hefeweizen. I laughed every time I looked at the artwork. Felix really captured Nolan's lumberjack essence with an illustration of him wearing a red plaid shirt while he held Norah in his arms. It fit the beer name perfectly.

I walked down to the dock, and Felix smiled at me when I handed him the beer. "Thanks."

I cocked my head as I studied the landscape painting he was working on. He was painting the lake in front of him, and it was fantastic. He was an amazing designer, so I wasn't surprised. I just didn't know he was also a talented painter.

I sat on the dock and dipped my feet into the water. "I didn't know you were a painter. It's amazing."

"Thanks. This beer's so good."

I nodded. "Yeah, I like it, and I'm an IPA girl."

"Ugh! IPAs are like the pumpkin spice latte for beer drinkers. Ya basic!"

"Am not!"

He set his paints down and sat on the dock next to me. I splashed him with my feet. ·

"Brat," he teased.

I felt heat rush up my cheeks at the memory of last night. He liked when I was a brat.

I held up the beer bottle and admired the label. "The artwork's perfect."

He studied his beer bottle and shrugged. "Not that hard to do. Nolan already exudes that whole hot lumbersexual thing."

I stared at him for what felt like forever.

"What?" he asked.

"You think Nolan's hot?"

He shrugged. "Still bi, Gemma!"

"I know that! Didn't see Nolan as your type."

He shrugged. "I call it like I see it."

Hmm, that was interesting.

He sighed. "Can we talk about last night?"

I shook my head.

"I'm sorry, Gemma. For everything. For standing you up and for leaving before you woke up. I'm not sorry for what we did together, though. We both enjoyed that. But I know I've been a dick to you."

I nodded. That was all true. I sipped my beer and kicked my feet in the water. I took my seashells out of my pocket and rubbed one between my fingers.

"Is there a reason?" I finally asked.

He took a big gulp of his beer. "What?"

"It's not because something's wrong with me, right?"

His face fell, and he set his beer down on the dock. He tipped my face up to look me in the eye. "No, absolutely not. Did you think that?"

"Fe, you cursed me."

He frowned. "What?"

"I haven't been able to hold down a date since you stood me up. If they don't ghost me, they don't show up. And then I let you seduce your way into my bed...twice."

Anger rose inside me at all the ways he had done me wrong. I kept letting him take advantage of me, and letting him into my heart, even though he stomped all over it.

"My dad's in jail," he said bitterly.

I pulled back at his admittance.

He picked at the label of his beer. "My dad's in jail for drug charges again, and I have custody of my little sister. Again. I've raised my sister since I was fourteen years old when my mom finally left us. That's why I stood you up, Gemma. I can't give you what you want from me, no matter how much I want it. So I'm an asshole to you because Skye's the most—"

"Why didn't you tell me that?" I shrieked at him without letting him finish his sentence.

"Because you wouldn't understand!"

"Of course I'd understand. I'm not a monster. If you told me you had a family emergency, I would have understood."

"Gemma, I can't commit to a relationship. Skye's my world. I'll always choose her over you. I've already done that before."

I looked out onto the lake and drank my beer in thought. I couldn't be mad at him, but he sounded a lot like Nolan right there. Declan said Nolan sacrificed a lot when their parents died, but he made himself out to be a martyr. Felix was doing the same thing, putting all the weight of the world on his shoulders when he didn't have to.

"Is that what happened with your ex?" I asked.

He nodded. "Roger was kinda needy, but he also wasn't out. We had to hide our relationship, and I couldn't deal."

"Because you're not ashamed of who you love."

He pointed at me. "Yup. I don't care who knows I'm bi. I hate the idea that straight's the default, like I have to make a big production about my sexuality."

"I get that," I said.

I might be a loud and proud bisexual woman, but I

understood what he meant. Why was straight always the default? Why did I have to amp myself up to tell my dad and sister I liked more than one gender?

He picked at his beer label. "It's taking me every ounce of control to not kiss you again right now. I want to do that so badly. I want to kiss you again and hold you in my arms and promise you the world. But I can't give you empty promises. It's unfair to you."

My heart thrummed. I wanted to kiss him again so badly, too, but he was right. I wanted a partner. I wanted someone to love me unconditionally. Someone to deal with eccentric Gemma Jensen, and love me despite my flaws. That person wasn't Felix.

So, I changed the subject instead. "What did you do today?"

"Went for a hike at the preserve and drew in my sketchbook. I wanted to paint the horizon."

"I didn't know you painted. I knew you were talented. Your artwork's amazing. I didn't expect to find you with a painting and an easel like a regular old Bob Ross."

He took another sip of his beer and glanced up at his work. "It's my first love. I closed my availability on my website so I didn't have any design work to do this week."

I cocked my head at him. "You don't just design for the brewery?"

He shook his head. "Nah. Declan actually encouraged me to start my business. I don't make a lot, but I love it, so it helps me keep food on the table."

"Fucking Declan," I muttered. He was such a busybody.

Felix ignored my muttering. "What did you do today? Catch anything good for dinner?"

I laughed. "Nah. Met up with an old friend from my childhood. We sunbathed and drove the boat around."

"I didn't know you had a boat."

I gave him a funny look. "How did you think I fished yesterday?"

He shrugged.

I held up a seashell. "After I docked, I walked down to the sand and picked shells. It's a tradition."

"There's a beach here?"

"It's a man-made lake. It's more woodsy back here than on the main dock."

"I like it here. What's the plan for tomorrow?"

"Want to do a brewery crawl with me?" I asked as an offering of peace. My heart might feel a little tender, but getting beers together could be the olive branch we both needed.

His lips curled up into a smile. "You want my company? Even after everything?"

I sighed. "Felix, I get why you did what you did. I'm still mad, but maybe buy me a good IPA and a beer hall pretzel, and I can forgive you."

He laughed. "That's all it takes?"

"I'm a simple gal."

"Liar."

I shrugged. "I gotta get a shower and wash all the sunblock off. I wish you had told me what was going on. I understand the burden on your shoulders. I mean, I don't, but I can imagine. That's a lot."

He nodded. "Thanks for understanding."

"Why didn't you bring your sister? I could have taught her how to fish and build a fire. Make her a real mountain woman."

"Her annual trip to Cape May with her best friend."

I frowned. "Oh. And now you're stuck with me."

He smirked. "If you behave, it's not so bad."

"Asshole!"

"You know it," he said, but he seemed sad about that. "Go get your shower, Gem. I'll grill up burgers for dinner and have a beer waiting for you."

"Aw, you feel awful about taking advantage of me."

He glared at me. "Umm no, you begged me to fuck you raw last night. Don't forget that, sweet thing."

I gave him the finger as I stood up and walked away. If I didn't, I'd kiss him again, and that wasn't a good idea. I tried to ignore his comment about how he wanted to kiss me. I couldn't let my hormones get the better of me a third time.

I was still mad at him, but I wasn't sure if I still hated him. I couldn't hate a man who dropped his whole life to take care of his little sister. Stepping up and being the parent when your parents couldn't hack it was admirable. It made sense why he and Nolan got along so well. They were cut from the same stubborn cloth. It also made him sexy as hell. Hot single dad, yes, please! I told my pussy to calm down because we couldn't do that again. My heart couldn't take it.

CHAPTER FOURTEEN

FELIX

I flipped burgers on the grill out on the porch and sipped my beer. I had a bottle of 611 Ale ready for Gemma when she came downstairs.

"Is that for me?" Gemma asked. She pointed toward the beer on the table a few feet away.

"Geez, Gem, you're sneaky. Yeah, it's for you."

"I thought you were kidding about having a beer waiting for me. You need help with dinner?"

"Nah. Sit that fine ass down. I got it."

It surprised me when she didn't argue, but sat down at the table while I finished dinner.

Telling her about my dad and Skye had been like a weight lifted off my shoulders, but it still didn't excuse my behavior, and a part of me wished she hadn't been so understanding. I'd rather she screamed in my face and told me it didn't matter because I was still a dick. That would have made things way easier. But no, sweet, little Gemma had to be nice and forgive me.

I turned off the grill and put the burgers on a paper plate. I joined Gemma at the table where I had laid out all the fixings for dinner. I sat next to her, and she grabbed a bun to assemble her burger. I heaped potato salad on my plate and squirted ketchup and mustard on my bun.

We ate in companionable silence, sipping our beers and enjoying being able to eat outdoors. Maybe I should have told her about Skye sooner.

"I think I'll make another fire tonight," she said after finishing her burger.

"Yeah? You want help this time?"

She shook her head. "Nah. I like doing it. Thanks for dinner."

I watched her take the dinner supplies back inside. She came outside a little while later and walked down to the fire pit to get the fire started. I joined her in front of the fire after getting us another round of beers. She gave me a smile as she took hers, but she was busy with something in her hands.

"What's that?" I asked.

"Oh. I make jewelry," she said.

"Oh. Like the one around your neck?"

She nodded. "Yup."

"Pretty. What do you do that for?"

She shrugged. "Fun. I have a store, but I don't make a lot off of it. It's mostly friends and family."

"What's it called?" I asked, and I took my phone out.

She grimaced. "Don't laugh."

"I won't."

Her expression didn't change. "Yes, you will."

"Just tell me."

"Gemma's Gems."

My shoulders shook as I tried not to laugh.

She kicked my foot. "I said not to laugh!"

"It's not terrible," I lied. I pulled up her craft shop and winced when I saw the terrible logo on her shop. It looked like she threw up the shop name in freaking PowerPoint. "Oh, Gem, let me make you a better logo."

"It's not a big deal," she said with a shrug and went back to fiddling with the jewelry in her hand.

I browsed her site, and I was impressed with the quality of the photos on each product. She had good ad copy, too. I checked her personal social media, and she did a good job promoting it. But she needed better artwork.

"Please?"

She arched a sculpted eyebrow at me. "Why?"

"You already know how to market yourself, but I can make you some kick-ass graphics."

"Again, why do you care?"

I gave her an annoyed look.

"Is that your idea of a peace offering? So I'll forgive you for being such a twat waffle?"

I took a sip of my beer instead of answering.

"Okay, but it better be good."

I pulled up the sleeve of my flannel and pointed out the artwork on my arm. "I design all my tattoos. I don't half-ass it with my art."

She held up her hands. "Okay, impress me, then."

"Oh, don't you worry, I will."

"Cocky!"

She laughed and put her work down to take another swig of her beer.

She set her beer down and got up to poke at the fire again. She put in more logs, but on her way back to her chair, she tripped over my feet. I reached an arm out and pulled her into my lap before she fell on her ass. Or worse, into the fire.

"Whoa there," I said.

A blush rose across her pale face. For a moment, time stood still as I cradled her in my arms, and she stared into my very soul. She slid her hands around my neck and bent her head to mine to meet me in a slow kiss.

When she kissed me, I forgot about all the reasons why this was a bad idea. I didn't stop her when she took the lead and ran her tongue across mine. Instead, I slid my hands up the back of her hoodie, my body tingling as I felt the warmth of her skin, and I kissed her harder. We kissed for so long the fire had died down when she pulled away.

She shifted, straddling me like she might ride my dick right here in front of the fire.

Don't think about that, Felix. Stop thinking about fucking her again.

"Fe?"

"Yeah?" I croaked out.

"Tell me to stop," she said as she rested her forehead against mine and her lips ghosted across mine. "Tell me you don't want to kiss me again."

I cupped her face and pulled back to take her all in. Her cheeks were flushed pink, and her lips were swollen from being kissed too much. And yet not enough. I wanted to kiss her all night long until she begged me to stop.

"Gem, I want to kiss you until you can't breathe. I want to take you inside and have my way with you until you're gasping for breath and can't handle one more orgasm. And then I want to give you one more."

She bit her lip, and then the little brat rubbed herself on my dick. Fuck me. She was going to be the end of me.

I gripped her hair in my fist. "I can only give you this week. I can't give you anything more."

She dipped her head back down and hovered over my mouth. "Give me this week. Fuck me until you break me, and come Sunday, we'll go home with nothing changed."

"I want something to change."

"What's that?" she asked and stared at me with eyes hooded with lust.

"After this week, you won't hate me anymore."

"No promises," she said and kissed me again.

We were kidding ourselves with these promises, but we were too horned up to think about the consequences. If she wanted a summer fling, I could give her that, but that was all I could give her. No matter how much I longed for something more.

"Come on!" Gemma's excitable voice cut through my dream. "Wake up, wake up, wake up!"

I put a pillow over my head as the too cheery woman bounced on my bed with a big grin on her face.

We had spent all night together in the big bedroom upstairs after Gemma doused the fire. And by all night, I meant marathon sex. I used my vibrating tongue ring on her multiple times and face fucked her before I pounded her tight little pussy until she screamed my name loud enough to wake every animal in the woods. It was the wee hours of the morning by the time we passed out naked in each other's arms.

How was she awake already?

"FELIX!" she whined.

"Sweet thing, please," I groaned.

She straddled me and tore the pillow off my face. I still wasn't awake, but my dick woke up to the sensation of her body on top of mine. "Wake up so we can do our brewery crawl!"

I completely forgot about that after spending the entire night with her in my arms. I kinda didn't want to leave this bed, but Gemma was a woman on a mission.

She shoved a map into my face where she had little 'X's marking what I assumed were all the breweries she wanted to tour today. Her eyes sparkled with excitement over her plan. Gemma might seem flighty, but people mistook her passion for airheadedness. She was so adorable when she got excited.

I pointed to my lips. "Gimme a kiss first."

She bent down to kiss me, and then I flipped her onto her back and took over.

"Felix! Later! I want to go drink beers and spy on other breweries."

I laughed into her neck. "The point of vacation is to not think about work."

"But let's go drink beer, Felix! You still owe me that IPA and a pretzel."

I groaned. "All right. If that gets you to behave."

She shimmied underneath me and gave me a naughty grin. Such a brat, but I loved it. "You know I don't behave."

I wrapped my hand around her throat. "You're such a brat. Do I need to teach you a lesson before I even have my coffee?"

She threw me off of her and jumped up out of bed. "Later! Get dressed and meet me downstairs. I'm making chocolate chip pancakes."

"Woman! Why didn't you lead with that?"

She gave me another cheeky grin before sprinting out of

the room. Gemma was unstoppable, and she wasn't someone who liked to do nothing on vacation. I liked that about her. It was cute how she was all go-go-go. I also liked how she knew her way around the woods and wasn't afraid to get down and dirty.

She was bouncing up and down in her seat when I joined her for breakfast. I gave her the stink eye while I sipped my coffee.

"You're excitable this morning," I grumbled, raking a hand through my bedhead.

"Don't be so grumpy! I only have a few days left of vacation, and I want to do ALL the things!"

"Okay, where are you dragging me today?" I asked. I cut into my pancakes and started eating while she filled me in on the plan for today.

She wanted to go to the brewery in town first. She didn't love their IPA, but she wanted to try their other beers. Then she had a couple more close by she wanted to try out.

"So, what do you think?" she asked.

"I'm game. Tomorrow, you want to teach me how to fish?"

Her bright blue eyes lit up like fireworks. "Seriously?"

"Yeah, girl. Teach me your mountain woman ways," I joked.

She got up and did a little dance, then planted herself in my lap. I slid my hands around her hips and held her to me.

She pressed her forehead to mine and gave me a quick kiss. "I'll take you out on the boat and teach you my ways on the water. Or we can go for a hike. I'm game for that too."

I smiled and kissed her again. We got lost in the feeling of each other, pressing close together so we could be one again. I pulled away, only to yank her shirt over her head. I tossed it on the floor and fingered her jeans while she kissed my neck.

"Felix," she sighed.

I gave her a sly grin. "If I can only have you for this week, I want to make it count. Now get your ass upstairs."

She pouted.

"Now, Gemma. Or I'll make you wait until tomorrow."

She whimpered. "Can you use the tongue ring again?"

She yelped as I picked her up and carried her upstairs. We didn't leave when she wanted to, but I don't think she cared when she was coming all over my tongue and screaming my name.

It was only vacation sex. I didn't have time for a relationship. Even if bubbly, pink-haired Gemma Jensen made me long for it.

CHAPTER FIFTEEN

GEMMA

*F*elix was bad news for me. He was trouble with a capital T. But as I smiled at him from over my beer glass, I wasn't thinking about any of that. I only had a few more days with him before we had to go back to reality, and I was going to enjoy it.

I was glad we had sex this morning before leaving for the breweries. I wanted to savor him. To remember how he made every inch of my body come alive. To catalog the way he looked at me when he grabbed my throat as he fucked me to an inch of my life. I kept telling my heart to slow down, that it was only sex, but I knew it was getting big ideas. I tamped those down as I drank more of my beer.

"What do you think?" Felix asked as he finished his beer.

This was our second stop. The first brewery in town hadn't impressed me. I didn't have high hopes since I didn't love their IPA, and they disappointed me with their other offerings. We ordered a flight at this one, and I liked their IPA way better.

"Better than the last place, but our beer's better."

"Beer snob," he joked.

I shrugged and downed the rest of my beer. I pulled up the beer name list I had in my notes app on my phone and started typing new ideas as they came. Nolan mentioned a potential Oktoberfest beer or a stout during Christmas, so I had some names rattling around in my brain. I looked up at the ceiling as I thought and then typed more ideas.

"What are you doing?" Felix asked.

"Nolan was talking about a new stout or Oktoberfest beer. I'm trying to come up with names."

He narrowed his eyes at me. He had questioned my 'forced vacation' comment before, and I was sure he noticed I had grumbled about Declan yesterday. I was hoping he would ignore that.

"What's the real reason you came to the cabin this week?" he asked.

I pretended I didn't hear him. I put my phone down and scanned the draft list again.

"Gem?"

"Hmm? Oh, we should get going to the next place."

Felix grabbed my hand. "Gemma."

I sighed. "Fine. Declan wants me to become the marketing director."

"I thought you already were."

I shook my head. "No. I do the social media because no one else can be trusted. I just had to fix one of April's posts. She didn't even use any hashtags, and there were a ton of misspellings."

He peered at me curiously.

I sighed. "Declan wants me to think about my career, so

he basically forced this vacation on me. Can we not talk about this?"

"Gem, how much have you thought about work since you got here?"

I stared down at the draft list in my hand. Every spare thought I had was about the brewery. Coming to tour these breweries wasn't just because I wanted to drink different beers; it was me researching our competition. It was seeing what everyone else was doing and thinking about how else we could promote the brewery.

Felix held up the draft list and pointed at the guest lines section where this brewery featured beers from other breweries. "What was the first thing you did when we sat down and looked at the draft list?"

"Said we should start doing guest lines," I muttered.

"Gem, I don't understand why you're fighting this. You come up with the best names for the beers, you give me clear creative briefs for the artwork, and you have literally not stopped thinking about how to improve the brewery's branding since you got here."

"Because I don't want to fail!"

He reached a hand out and squeezed mine. "You won't. Declan can be a pain in the ass, but he sees your potential. That's why he wants you as his marketing director. He wouldn't pressure you if he didn't think you could do it."

I sighed. "But I failed before. I don't want all the pressure."

"Sweet thing."

I glared at him. "I had a fucking mental breakdown, okay? I had a high-pressure corporate marketing job, and I failed so spectacularly that Avery had to physically pull me out of my bed. I don't want to go through that again."

It was pissing me off that no one seemed to get why I

didn't want this job. Why it terrified me so much to fail Declan and Nolan. Avery saw the hell I went through, and she was pressuring me, too. Anxiety wound tight around my throat at the thought of that happening again.

Felix reached out and squeezed my hand. "Gem—"

"Can we stop talking about work?" I cut him off, interrupting whatever inspirational platitude he was about to say. "Let's go to the next brewery. You still owe me that pretzel."

I stormed off before he could say anything else, striking the conversation dead. That was rude of me, but I didn't want to talk about it anymore. I leaned up against Felix's car as I waited for him. He was taking his sweet time, but I didn't blame him. I left him with the check like a dick.

I checked my phone again and stared in confusion when I noticed someone had logged me out of the brewery's accounts. Shit, I hoped someone hadn't gotten our password. I was going to do a 'forgot password' when a text popped up.

DEC: *If you're gonna work on your vacation, just take the job, Gem!*

I scowled and typed back.

ME: *I don't WANT it.*

DEC: *Take the fricking job, Gem!*

I was typing back a nasty reply when a dark shadow came across my vision. I looked up and saw Felix standing in front of me. He tilted up my chin, and I forgot what I was doing when he slanted his mouth on mine.

I moaned into his mouth as he kissed me softly in the parking lot. He kissed me like he wanted to savor the sensation of his lips on mine. Like he didn't want to let go.

His dark brown eyes sparkled underneath the bright

summer sunshine when he pulled away. "Am I being pushy, or are you being stubborn?" he asked.

"Yes."

He laughed and cupped my jaw in his rough hands. "Think about it, Gem. You're so good at what you do. It's perfect for you."

"Can we please stop talking about this?" I whined and slid my phone back into my pocket. I couldn't believe Declan had changed all the passwords on me. What a controlling asshat.

"Okay, but you're hangry, so let's eat at the next brewery."

A grin spread across my face. "I still want a big pretzel!"

He smiled as he walked around to the driver's side of the car. I slid into the passenger seat, and we went on our way. He surprised me when he grabbed my hand in his when we got on the road. He brought my hand up to his lips and kissed it. It was a sweet gesture, but something you did when you were in a relationship. Not a summer fling. My heart was doing backflips inside my chest, and I tried to tell it not to get excited. It was only for this week. Then Felix would go back to being the single-dad martyr he felt he needed to be.

It was a short drive to the next brewery, which was hopping because it was the height of summer, and it was lunchtime. I *was* kinda hungry. We sat at the bar, and I perused the menu before a bartender came over to us.

"Want to split the pretzel?" I asked after Felix ordered a flight for us to share. "I need to eat an actual lunch."

"I'm down for that. The burger looks good."

"I kinda want to get wings. But don't laugh when I make a mess of it."

He leaned into me, his lips on my ear. "I love when you make a mess."

I bit my lip to keep in the whimper. "Fe," I whined.

He kissed my neck and then moved away.

Such an asshole!

We ordered food, and I scanned the menu. "Oh, this one has guest lines, too. Hmmm."

He laughed into his beer glass. "You're thinking about it for our brewery, aren't you?"

"Yeah...it's not a bad idea."

He finished the beer he was sampling and offered me the hoppy pale ale. I took a tiny sip. It was good, but I still loved Area 267 better. Maybe I was biased.

The bartender came over and dropped off the pretzel for us to share. "Did I hear you guys work for a brewery?"

Felix nodded. "Yeah, but we're out in Philly."

Drakesville, Philly, close enough.

"Oh, what's the name?" the bartender asked. He was a bigger guy with a trimmed beard, and he looked familiar to me, but I couldn't place why.

"MacGregor Brothers Brewing Company," I said.

The bartender nodded and smiled. "Oh, Nolan's gig. Yeah, I know Nolan. He's a good guy." He pulled a card out and handed it to Felix. "If you're ever interested in doing a guest line, have Nolan or Declan call me."

Felix handed the card to me. "I'll have our new marketing director handle that."

I glared at him but pocketed the card.

"Well, enjoy guys!" he said and walked away.

"Why did you do that?" I snapped.

Felix shrugged. "Eat your pretzel and be quiet."

I glared at him. "You're only allowed to tell me what to do in bed."

He winked at me. "Yeah, I do like that about you."

"Asshole," I muttered under my breath.

I tore off a piece of pretzel, dipped it into the beer cheese, and shoved it into my mouth. I knew he was trying to help, but I didn't want it. Why couldn't he understand that?

We ate lunch and ordered another flight while I made a mess of my wings.

Felix handed me a pile of napkins and hand wipes when I finished. I wiped my mouth, a little embarrassed that I let myself eat them like an animal. Felix smiled at me and doodled on his napkin.

"What's that?" I asked.

He showed me a design with a crystal wrapped around some flowers. "Just tinkering."

"Is that for my shop?" I asked.

He nodded and pocketed the napkin. "I need to think about it. Maybe add a banner with your shop name on it."

"Do you think it's a terrible name?" I asked. I came up with the name on the fly. It told people exactly what they were getting when they ordered jewelry from me.

"It's growing on me."

"You don't have to do that."

He ran a finger across his eyebrow piercing, and he furrowed his brow. That was Felix's thinking face. "I want to. I can't help wanting to make something beautiful for you. To reflect you."

Butterflies flew around in my stomach at his words. "Thank you," I whispered.

The bartender dropped off the check, and Felix didn't let me even pretend to fight him over it. I would get the next round.

"Where to next?" he asked.

I held up one finger. "One more, and then you're free to go."

He waggled his eyebrows. "What if I don't want to be free to go?"

I shrugged. "I can think of something."

He grinned at me. "I've got some ideas."

CHAPTER SIXTEEN

FELIX

I slapped Gemma's ass as she rolled her hips and rode me.

"Ride my fucking dick, sweet thing," I growled beneath her.

She nodded and pressed her hands against my chest. I swiped my thumb across her needy clit, and she shuddered while she rode me harder. I lifted my knees up behind her to get better leverage as I topped her from the bottom. She leaned back, and I watched my dick sliding in and out of her pussy.

Fuck, that was a beautiful sight.

"Fuck, fuck, fuck," she moaned while her movements above me got more frantic. Our bodies slapped together, and she shook when she came all over my dick.

"That's it, sweet thing," I purred beneath her but didn't stop fingering the bud of her clit.

"Felix," she moaned as she slumped onto my chest.

I held her hips down and bucked up inside her. She felt

so good with her inner walls squeezing around my dick. Not as good as when she let me go bare inside her, but we both agreed condoms were a must. Coming on her tits had been hot as fuck, but it was too dangerous to do that again.

She kissed my neck as she lay on my chest, trying to catch her breath after her last orgasm. "Come for me," she whispered in my ear. "Come inside this pussy like you own it."

Fuck me. She knew the shit that got me going.

I slapped her ass. "Mine," I growled.

"Yours," she agreed as she sucked on my neck.

I pushed her back up to a seated position. "Let me see those tits bounce while I come inside you."

She nodded while she rode me again, and when she brought her hands up to play with her tits, I was a goner. I reached a hand up and wrapped it around her throat. "Mine," I growled again. Then I came so hard, I felt like I was having an out-of-body experience. The pussy was *that* good.

I loosened my grip on her neck and flopped back down on the bed. She lifted herself off of me gently so she didn't dislodge the condom and lay down next to me. I lay there for a couple seconds in silence, and then I took the condom off and tossed it in the trash.

She nudged her head into my chest, and I pulled an arm around her. She cuddled into my chest, and a sense of warmth spread throughout my whole body while I played with her hair. It was so nice to fuck her until we both couldn't speak. To have her in my arms afterward and pretend I could have something more after this week. But I couldn't. Spending the day with her on her brewery crawl had been a bad idea.

She looked up at me. "Felix?"

"Hmm?"

"You're really quiet."

I kissed her quickly. "Pussy so good it melted my brain."

She laughed. It boomed across the room and reminded me of how this bubbly woman lit up any room she was in.

"I didn't expect this," she admitted.

"What?"

"That we'd have sex again when I discovered you here. Or that you'd appease me on my brewery tour."

"It was fun."

I didn't bring up the job opportunity again. She was mad at me for telling the guy at the brewery she was the marketing director. But the past couple of days, she made little comments about stuff she wanted to do for the brewery like she was already doing the job. She deserved the promotion, and I didn't understand why she thought she'd fail at it.

"You really want me to teach you to fish tomorrow?" she asked.

I laughed. "Uhh, I don't know if I want to fish, but show me the lake. Show me what you like to do here."

"Well... I can take you out on the boat. We'll pack lunch and have a day out on the water. Or we can have a day on the sandy lake. Or we can go kayaking."

That all sounded nice.

"Whatever you want."

She looked up at me with a mischievous grin. "Do you know what I want right now?"

I grinned because I knew what the little nympho wanted.

She rubbed her thumb across my beard. "I want to ride your beard again."

I raised an eyebrow. "I'm not stopping you."

"While you use your tongue ring."

I grinned. "Oh, you love that thing, huh?"

"Felix!" she laughed. "It's like you have a vibrator in your mouth. It feels amazing."

I turned it on and felt the vibrations in my mouth. "Good thing I packed extra batteries. Get up here and ride my tongue."

I didn't have to tell her twice.

A couple of hours and a shower later, Gemma stood in the kitchen, peering into the fridge. I sat on the couch with my sketchbook in hand, working on the logo for her jewelry store. I liked where this was going, but it wasn't complete. I still needed to transfer it to my computer.

"What's wrong?" I asked.

"What should we do for dinner?" she asked. "I don't feel like cooking."

I didn't either. I was beat from both our brewery crawl and all the sex we had afterward.

"There's frozen pizza in the freezer," I said.

"Let's go out," she said.

"We were out all day," I argued.

"Please, Felix," she begged.

"You're such a brat," I muttered.

She bounded over to the couch and jumped into my arms. She gave me that pouty look I couldn't say no to. "We can go over to the resort. They have a great bar on the dock. It's so nice. And I've known one of the bartenders since I was a small child."

She was so cute when she got all excited. "You're a brat because when you give me that pouty face, I can't say no."

"Please! I want some good-ass crab cakes."

I laughed. "Is that what they're called?"

She nodded. "Uh-huh."

I slid her off my lap. "Okay, let me change."

She was wearing a black dress with bright pink flowers that matched her hair. She looked ready to go, while I was lounging on the couch in a pair of jeans and a ratty t-shirt. She glanced at my sketchbook in between us on the couch. She studied it for a moment. "Is this the logo for me?"

I nodded. "It's just a sketch. I added the banner for your shop over the crystal. I gotta draw it into my program and colorize it."

She played with the crystal at her neck. "Can you make it a rose quartz?"

I nodded. "That was my plan. What do you think so far?"

Her smile lit up the entire room, and it struck me that Gemma had never smiled at me like that before. It wasn't her bright customer service smile either; it was a genuine smile from her. I pressed a hand to my chest, as if she had struck me there. I tried to shove all that down.

I had asked out Gemma last year because I wanted to get to know her. She was excitable and fun to be around, and my dad seemed like he was finally on the right track. Finding my sister crying on the couch after I first slept with Gemma reminded me why my sister had to be my sole focus. But there was a part of me that wondered, what if I didn't have to sacrifice my happiness for my sister? Wondered if I could have it all.

Gemma held my sketchbook to her chest. "Fe, I love it!"

"Am I forgiven yet?" I asked. She put her finger on her chin and pretended to be in thought. I reached over and tickled her. "Am I?"

She giggled uncontrollably as she squirmed underneath me. "STOP!"

I shook my head. "Nuh-uh, not until you answer the question."

"I guess."

"You guess? Would it help if I gave you more orgasms?"

A sly smile curled around her lips. "Maybe...but dinner first! Your girl's hungry."

I smiled at the idea of her being my girl, of this wild and adventurous woman being someone I could keep. Only in my dreams.

"Okay, okay. Let me get dressed," I said and went upstairs.

I put on a button-down and grinned when I saw Gemma's reflection in the bathroom mirror.

"You don't have to dress that nice," she said. She slid her arms around my waist and kissed my neck.

"You look so cute in that dress. I can't go to dinner in my ratty t-shirt."

She moved away from me and did a little twirl. "This old thing?"

"It matches your hair," I said as I combed out my beard and then my hair.

She grinned and exaggeratedly put her hands in the pockets. "Thanks. It has pockets!"

I didn't know what it was about women, but they loved to tell you that either their dress had been on sale or it had pockets. Sometimes both.

"Come on, pockets, let's roll," I said.

"I'll drive," she offered.

We drove to the other side of the lake to the crowded bar near the resort. We sat outside waiting for a table, and I slid my hand into Gemma's on reflex. Her hand fit into mine like we were two pieces of a puzzle locking into place. I needed to stop thinking we could have anything outside of the next couple of days. This thing between us stayed at the lake. We couldn't bring it back to Drakesville.

We didn't have to wait long until the host sat us outside on the dock with a view of the lake. It was nice to feel the breeze on our faces as we scanned the menu. I ordered a beer, but Gemma stuck with lemonade because she said she drank too much at the breweries earlier. True, but I wouldn't tell her that.

"What's good here?" I asked.

"Crab cakes, crab cakes," she chanted.

I felt a smile tug at my lips at her excitement. I scanned the menu and then closed it. We both ordered the crab cakes and relaxed into a comfortable silence.

I took a sip of my beer and watched her close her eyes as the wind whipped in her hair. She looked so beautiful and at peace that I couldn't help myself. I took my phone out and snapped a photo of her.

One blue eye snapped open, and she gave me a suspicious look. "Did you just take a picture of me?"

"You told me to."

Both her eyes opened, and she gave me a confused look. "Huh?"

"You said, 'Take a picture, it will last longer.'"

She erupted into laughter. "I forgot about that. That feels like ages ago."

I shook my head. Maybe it felt like ages, but it hadn't been. Not quite. It reminded me of how little time I had with her. The lake would be our dream world, and in a couple of days, all of it would be behind us.

She looked like she wanted to ask what was on my mind, but then the server brought out our dinner. We dug in, and Gemma moaned as she ate. I had to shift my dick in my pants at the sound of it.

When I took my first bite, I understood why she made that noise. And then I laughed.

"What's so funny?" she asked.

"These are good-ass crab cakes," I said with a smirk.

She laughed again, and at that moment, I loved that I made her laugh. She wasn't glaring at me or telling me to go fuck myself. Even though I deserved all of that. On this dock, Gemma Jensen was wearing a pretty dress and smiling at me like I never did anything wrong.

"Told you they were good," she said with a cute, cocky grin.

"They are."

We chatted while we finished our dinner, and Gemma was patient while I sipped my beer. We watched the water as the sun went down, and it reeked like this was a date.

"You're forgiven," she said after some time passed.

"Hmm?"

She gave me a bright smile. "For standing me up."

I quirked up my eyebrow. "Oh?"

She nodded. "Letting me drag you to all those breweries and dinner tonight made up for it. But, Felix..."

"Yeah?"

She pressed her lips together in thought. "I would have understood if you told me about your family situation. I think it's amazing you took the reins in raising your sister. But it doesn't mean you can't have a love life."

I wished that were true, but I had already tried with Roger, and I chose Skye over him. I didn't want to do that to Gemma. She deserved to be on a pedestal.

"I just can't."

She nodded, but the way she looked down at her phone and ignored me told me I had said the wrong thing.

I wanted to say something else, but then two women walked over to our table. I recognized the one woman as the cheery blonde barista from the coffee shop. She was holding hands with a tall, Black woman with natural curls.

"Hey, Gemma!" the blonde said.

Gemma gave them both a bright smile. "Hey, Harper, Keisha. How are you?"

"Good," the Black woman said and then looked over at me. "Oh, I'm Keisha. This is my wife, Harper."

I held out a hand and shook both of theirs. "Felix. I know your wife from the coffee shop."

The blonde looked up at the sky. "Felix. Black coffee and a pastry. Right?"

I laughed. "You got it."

Gemma scoffed. "So boring. What are you two up to?"

"Just got done with dinner," Harper said.

"Us too," I told her.

"Hey, what are you up to tomorrow?" Keisha asked. "We're both off, so we're doing a day at the lake."

Gemma looked at me before answering. "We haven't decided."

Keisha looked curiously at me and then back to Gemma. I wasn't sure what that meant.

"Gem, you want to have a day at the lake? I'm game," I said.

Gemma clapped her hands excitedly. "Okay! We can go out on the boat later."

"Whatever you want."

"We'll see you tomorrow, then!" Harper said. "We gotta get going."

We waved goodbye to them, and then the server

brought over our check. Gemma grabbed it from out of my hands and wouldn't let me pay. She insisted on going out for dinner, so I'd let that slide. For now.

We didn't linger at the restaurant for too much longer. When we got back to the cabin, Gemma put on music and cleaned up the kitchen while I got my laptop out and started working on her logo. I was loving this design for her shop. It fit her personality, especially if you knew Gemma was tattooed with flowers on her body. Tattoos I loved to kiss one by one.

"Is that the final design?" she asked when she came back into the living room.

"Not finished yet. I want to tinker some more."

"Can I see it again?"

"Nope."

She pouted.

I shook my head and lifted her up in my arms. "Nope, that's not gonna work on me tonight. Let's go to bed."

We didn't even have sex when we crawled into the bed together. We were both wiped out from our adventure today. Instead, we lay in bed together, watching something random on TV.

I shouldn't have brought her up here with me. We should have gone to bed separately. Lying in bed watching trashy tv together was something you did with your partner, not the woman you said you couldn't commit to and agreed to have a vacation fling with.

Was I a complete dumbass for doing this?

"Felix?" she asked.

"Hmm?" I murmured and stroked her hair.

"Thanks for appeasing me today."

"It was fun."

She smiled up at me and gave me a sweet kiss goodnight. I turned off the TV and shut the light off. I rolled her onto her side and held her tight against my chest as we fell asleep.

I thought I could try with Gemma. Maybe I *could* give her and Skye the time they both needed.

CHAPTER SEVENTEEN

GEMMA

I hummed as I made our sandwiches and packed snacks into the cooler. Felix was still upstairs tinkering with my logo, so I was getting our bags together for our day out on the lake. The past couple of days had been fun, but I was trying not to think about how little time we had left. I shouldn't have slept in his bed last night. That felt so relationship-y, and this was just a fling. No matter how much sexual chemistry we had.

I threw in fruit and crackers and took the cooler out to the car. Then I went into the garage, got out the beach chairs and umbrella, and put them into the trunk of my car. Felix came outside in his board shorts and t-shirt.

"You need help?" he asked.

I waved him off. "Nah, I got it. You ready?"

He nodded. "You got the sunblock, right?"

I walked over to the driver's side of the car. "Yes!"

"Snacks? Water?"

I rolled my eyes at him. "Yes, Dad! Let's go."

He laughed. "Sorry, I'm being a dad, aren't I?"

"An annoying ass, more like it," I muttered under my breath. The salty look he gave me told me he heard me.

We drove over to the sandy lake near the resort, and Felix helped me drag all our stuff over to a nice spot in the sand. This was why I preferred going out on the boat or hiking. Going to the lake was such a production.

Felix set up the umbrella and chairs while I laid down the beach blanket. I shimmied out of my shorts and took off my shirt so I could put on my sunblock. Felix had already taken off his shirt, and his tattoos gleamed in the bright summer sun. He stared at me for a second, and I knew it was because I was wearing the skimpiest bikini I owned. That might have been intentional.

"You want help?" he asked when he picked his jaw up from the sand.

I gave him a sultry look from over my shoulder. "I can't reach my back."

I snickered when he swore under his breath, but he sat behind me and rubbed sunblock into his hands. He moved my hair out of the way and smeared the sunblock down my back. His rough hands felt so good on my skin that I forgot where I was.

"Gemma, stop moaning," he growled in my ear when he stopped.

"Sorry, I like your hands on me."

He pressed a kiss to my shoulder. "I know, sweet thing. I can get my hands all over you again later."

"You had me this morning!" I teased.

Waking up in bed with him meant we took advantage of that. I wanted to make use of his body if I had limited time with it. Especially since I was pretty sure I'd go back to being dateless Gemma when we got back to Drakesville.

I put the rest of my sunblock on and did Felix's back for him in return. I put my shades on and lay back on the blanket to catch some rays. Honestly? Laying at the lake was kinda boring, but I'd get in the water after Keisha and Harper got here.

I lifted my sunglasses at the sound of footsteps in the sand, and jumped up when the girls came over to us. Keisha plopped down their chairs while Harper laid down their blanket next to mine.

"Hey!" I said to them. "You made it."

"Oh my god, Gem, go in the water. I know you're itching to," Harper said.

"You want help?" Felix asked them as they were setting up.

They waved him off, and I dragged him off to join me down at the water. My feet pounded into the sand as I ran into the lake. The lake was man-made, but they brought in sand to give it that beachy feel. Some people didn't like the idea of swimming in these lakes, but I always loved it. I spent my childhood swimming in this lake, and I always loved coming back to it.

Felix caught up to me in the water and swung me around in his arms. I wrapped my legs around his waist underneath the water and leaned my head back when he twirled me around.

"I didn't know you were so adventurous," he said. "I feel like since you busted your way into the cabin, you have been go-go-go."

"I like to do things. I'm not Avery."

He raised an eyebrow. "What's that mean?"

I laced my hands behind the back of his neck and clung to him like a little monkey. "Avery just wants a different room to read in. They came up here in the winter when she was pregnant, and she did nothing! Winter can be fun because you can ski or snowboard and stuff, but she was pregnant, and Nolan barely let her lift a finger."

Felix smiled. "They probably had a bunch of sex. It was their honeymoon."

I laughed. "True. Avs let it slip that he chopped a lot of firewood for her."

"So he is like a regular lumberjack!"

We laughed together.

Felix frowned. "Wait, does that mean they fucked in that bed as much as we have?"

I laughed. "Um...Felix, baby, my parents probably fucked in that bed too."

He shivered. "That doesn't bother you?"

I shook my head. "Nah. Dad always told me sex wasn't anything to be ashamed of. He didn't do that 'not till you're thirty' bullshit or the 'don't have sex or you'll get pregnant and die' thing. He told me what was what and then asked if I had questions."

He frowned.

"What's wrong?" I asked and framed his face with my hands.

"I worry about not teaching Skye enough. I tried, but she told me she had the internet and school had already taught her. I also might have told her no one should give her hickeys until she was thirty."

"How old is she?"

"Thirteen."

Thirteen? I thought she was much younger from the way he talked about her.

"She knew you were joking, right?"

He nodded.

"Then she knows you're just looking out for her."

I swam out of his arms.

"Where are you going?" he asked.

"Race me to the rope?" I asked.

He grinned. "You're on, Jensen!"

We splashed around in the lake until my fingers pruned and I wanted to eat lunch. Felix raced me back to the blanket, where we almost knocked over Harper.

Harper shook her head with a laugh. "Same old, Gemma!"

I shrugged. "Who goes to the lake and doesn't go in it?"

Keisha shuddered. "I don't know what's in there."

"Yeah!" Harper agreed with her wife. "What if I get sucked into the deep by Nessie?"

"Nessie? Like the Loch Ness Monster, who's one hundred percent not real?" Felix asked.

"She's real!" Keisha insisted.

I sat on the beach blanket, and Felix wrapped my towel around me while he dried himself off. I opened the cooler and unwrapped a ham and cheese sandwich for myself and handed him his. He sat next to me on the blanket while we ate our lunch.

Harper gave me the type of look you'd give a cute puppy.

"What?" I asked.

"You two are cute!" Keisha said.

I felt heat against my face, and it wasn't just from the hot afternoon sun. I shoved my sandwich in my face so I didn't have to say anything. I heard my phone vibrate, and I pulled it out and saw a text from Declan.

DEC: *Have you decided yet?*

I rolled my eyes, and unfortunately, Felix noticed.

"What's up?" he asked.

"Nothing," I said as I shoved my phone back into my bag and out of the direct sunlight.

"Tell me," he urged.

"Declan."

"Does this have to do with your forced vacation?" Harper asked.

I furrowed my brow at her.

Keisha swatted her wife's leg. "Babe! I told you to stop eavesdropping at the coffee shop."

She must have overheard my conversation with Avery on the phone. I was probably being loud, so I didn't blame her for listening.

They looked at Felix for an explanation. He sighed. "They offered her a promotion, and it's a great opportunity, but she turned it down. Our boss made her take a vacation to think about it."

"Why don't you want it?" Harper asked.

"That's what I asked," Felix said and nudged me.

"It's too much pressure," I explained. I glared at Felix. Even after I had admitted about my mental breakdown, he was still pushing me, and that pissed me off.

"But she's good at it. She hasn't stopped thinking about work since she got here. Or posting stuff on our social media. Except for yesterday," Felix said.

I shook my head. "That's because Dec changed the passwords on me."

"It sounds like you're already doing the job then, no?" Harper asked.

Felix pointed at her. "Yes, she is! And she's good at it. But she's stubborn."

"I don't want to talk about this," I said.

I got up and walked down toward the water to get away

from their prodding. I picked seashells as I walked and thought about my career.

The idea of failing the brewery made me break out in hives. I didn't want to see the look of disappointment on Declan's face when he realized giving me the job was a mistake. I didn't want to spend weeks depressed in bed because I couldn't measure up to the responsibility. But Felix had a point. The whole time I'd been here, all I thought about was marketing strategy for the brewery. I was already doing the job I claimed I didn't want.

But what if Declan fired me when I fucked up? Then I could never work at the brewery again.

I chewed on my lip and walked down the shoreline, collecting more shells in my hand as I did. The sun beat down on my body, but it felt good. I tried to put out positive vibes into the universe, begging it to give me a sign to tell me what to do. About both the job and the situation with Felix.

Here was the truth. I had fallen in love with him. Was it too soon? Absolutely. But in the past couple of days, he had shown me the real Felix. When he came to check on me during the storm, he showed his caring side. Now that I knew he sacrificed his own happiness to care for his little sister, it made me like him even more. I realized the age difference between them meant he had probably been doing that since he was her age. But that didn't mean he couldn't have a love life. Maybe he just didn't want that with me. Maybe his sister was just his excuse.

I didn't want kids, and maybe marriage wasn't on the table for me, but I wanted to find love. I wanted to find a partner who loved me for me. For all my eccentricities. I was a fool to think there was any future with Felix. He said he could only give me this week, but I wanted more. My heart wanted forever, and I was having a hard time telling it that wasn't an option.

I picked more seashells until my hands got full, and I had to walk back up to the blanket. Felix wasn't on the blanket anymore, so I sat on it and looked through my collection.

"I see you're doing the summer fling thing," Harper said.

I nodded.

"He's cute," Keisha said.

I nodded again.

"Oh, honey, did you catch feelings already?" Harper asked.

I nodded. "I think I had them a long time ago. I think that's why I pretended I hated him for so long. But I found out why he did everything."

"Why?" they asked.

"He has custody of his little sister, and he says he can't give someone the time they need."

Both women gave me a sympathetic look. Harper squeezed my arm. "Talk to him. When are you going home?"

"Sunday, but it's already Friday. I don't think I'll convince him we could be more. I knew my heart couldn't take this. I shouldn't have bothered."

"Maybe he'll change his mind."

Felix walked up from being in the lake, so I clamped my mouth shut. He sat behind me on the blanket and wrapped his arms around my waist. "Find anything good?" he asked.

I melted into him when he kissed my neck sweetly. I would worry about the fact I had caught feelings in such a short time when I got home. Right now, I gave in to the feeling of being in his arms.

I held up one of the good ones. "This one's good."

"Pretty. Maybe you should make nautical jewelry too."

"I was thinking about it. But I'd have to rename my shop."

"Ooh you have a shop, gimme!" Keisha said.

I told her the name, and she looked it up. "Ooh, girl, these are pretty. I'm buying some."

"We can change out the logo if you want to change the name. I'm not done with it yet, anyway," Felix said.

"Okay," I muttered.

"You okay?" he asked.

I nodded but changed the subject to lighten the mood. "Hey! What are you two doing tonight? Come over for a fire."

Harper's face brightened. "Oh my god, yes. Just like old times!"

"Except my dad won't catch us with the booze," I joked.

Harper smiled. "Ha! Your dad was probably the coolest, though. He just went, 'Okay, but don't cry to me when you're praising the porcelain god.' Your dad's a hoot."

I smiled. I loved my dad, and he certainly was that. "But seriously, come over. I'll make us a fire, and we can make s'mores. It will be like old times."

"But with more alcohol!" Harper joked.

I laughed and squinted at her. "Um, maybe less. We were animals as teens. Maybe Avs is right, Dad let me be feral."

We both erupted into laughter, and for a second, I forgot what I was worried about.

CHAPTER EIGHTEEN

FELIX

Gemma leaned back into my chest, and I kissed her temple. She didn't want to talk about the job stuff, but I felt like she needed the push. If Declan told her to take a vacation to think about it, she had to actually do that. I wasn't sure why she decided she wouldn't be good at it when she was already doing the job. I understood her awful experience before, but she poured everything into marketing the brewery. There was no way she could fail. Declan wouldn't let her, and neither would I.

I half-listened to the three women as they chattered on. I had some suspicions about Gemma's relationship with Harper, but I'd ask her about that later. Right now, my thoughts were loud in my head again. My heart was trying to convince me that maybe Gemma and I had a shot. But I didn't want to break her heart again.

"Hey," her voice pulled me out of my brooding thoughts.

I looked down at her, and her bright eyes stared up at me in confusion. "Where'd you go?"

I gave her a quick kiss. "I'm right here."

"I want to go back into the water," she said.

"Okay."

I watched her walk down to the lake and felt eyes on me. I turned and saw Harper and Keisha both giving me a hard look.

"What's up?"

"Felix," Harper began. "Do you have feelings for Gemma?"

I picked at a thread on the blanket. Yes, I did. I probably had for a long time. Gemma and I had only agreed to this fling two days ago. It was too soon to fall in love. But what if I already had those feelings and getting to know her these past couple of days unearthed them? It was all very confusing.

"Yeah," I finally said.

"Then you should do something about it," Harper said firmly.

I'd have loved to, but I couldn't. They wouldn't understand the pressure to be the provider. I had to make sure my sister had a roof over her head and food on the table. Being a single dad was hard, especially when that kid wasn't even yours, but you'd do anything to protect her.

I felt my phone buzz next to me, and I took it out of the beach bag and saw my sister calling me. My heart jumped into my throat.

"Hey, half pint, what's wrong?" I asked.

Skye laughed on the other end of the phone. "Nothing's wrong, you just haven't texted me eight million times, so I'm checking you're not dead."

"Half pint!"

She giggled. "Are you having a good vacation?"

I watched Gemma walking out of the lake. She flipped her soaking wet hair out of her face and walked toward our blanket. She was wearing the skimpiest string bikini that matched the bright color of her hair. She totally wore it on purpose, and it was doing wonders for me.

"Yeah, I am. You being good for the Parks?" I asked my sister.

"Of course! Ryan said to tell you to not be a dumbass and mess up with Gemma."

I clenched my teeth together. "He did?"

"Who's Gemma?"

I sighed. "A friend. She works at the brewery with me. When did you talk to Ryan?"

"He's here for the rest of the weekend. He said Gemma's with you at the cabin. Is she the one with pink hair?"

"That's the one."

"Big bro, she's cute. So I agree with Ry. Don't mess it up!"

I laughed. "Okay, if you say so. What else did Ryan tell you?"

"Nothing!"

Yeah, I knew a lie when I heard one. I'd have a talk with Ryan about that when I got home. It was bad enough that Avery and Declan meddled in my love life. I didn't need Ry doing it too.

Gemma walked up to the blanket and dried herself off with her towel. She gave me a curious look, and I mouthed, "My sister." She nodded in understanding but sat in between my legs, anyway. I wrapped my arms around her waist while I continued to chat with my sister.

"Tell Gemma I think her hair's pretty. And you'd look cute together!" Skye exclaimed.

I sighed. "Half pint!"

"What? I'm not a baby anymore, Fe-fe. I want you to be happy."

I ignored her. "When are you coming home? I want to make sure I'm at the house before you."

"We might stay a little longer, into next week."

"Okay, I'm coming home on Sunday, so I'll be waiting."

"Bye, big bro!" she said, then hung up on me. Teenagers, they could be so blunt.

Gemma looked up at me. "She thinks we'd be cute together?"

I rubbed a hand down my beard. "You heard that?"

She nodded but then looked down at her hands in her lap.

"Because you *are* cute!" Keisha exclaimed.

I wanted to believe Skye was right, but every time I dropped my guard, something bad happened. I wasn't sure I could take the chance.

Gemma sat up and took her phone out. "Take a selfie with me."

I appeased her with the photo and even let her take one with me kissing her neck. This woman was a ball of energy. She was bright and in your face, but when she smiled down on you, everything felt right.

Gemma was fidgeting. "What's wrong?" I asked.

"I'm kinda bored now."

I laughed. "I thought the plan was to relax at the lake?"

Harper laughed. "Gemma flits from one thing to the next. Go on. We'll catch up with you later!"

"You'll come over for a fire, right?" Gemma asked. "We leave in two days, so it's either tonight or tomorrow night."

149

Harper nodded. "We'll come over tonight. Go on, get out of here!"

Gemma jumped up and wrapped her towel around her. I helped her pack up, and we took everything over to the car, then walked over to the dock. I grabbed my sketchbook and pencil out of the beach bag at the last minute.

"What are we doing, Gem?" I asked.

I followed her to a boat tied up on the dock. She undid the moorings and got in. "Get in. I'm cruising you around the lake."

I smiled and hopped into the boat. "Okay. Can I drive?"

"Nope, you need a boating license, which I have, and you don't, so sit."

I sat down in one of the seats and laid my head back on the headrest. She drove us around the lake, and I enjoyed the ride. The wind whipped through my hair and it felt so damn peaceful. Gemma was humming to herself in the driver's seat. Back on the lake, I felt a sadness come over her, but she seemed okay now.

"You really think I'd be good as the marketing director?" she asked when she parked the boat out in the middle of the lake.

What kind of question was that? Of course I did.

I opened my eyes and found her sitting next to me. She bit her lip and looked uncharacteristically nervous.

I grabbed her hand and brought the back of it up to my lips. "Yes. You'd be amazing at it."

"Declan asked if I have an answer."

I pulled her into my lap and cupped her face. "Why don't you want it?"

She laced her hands behind my head. "I told you what happened the last time I had a high-pressure job. Not all of us want to be successful. Some of us just want to enjoy life."

I frowned at that. "What happened?"

"I told you, I had a mental breakdown."

"No. What happened?"

She sighed. "My boss constantly disrespected me. She'd say one thing, and then I'd do it, and I'd get 'this isn't what we talked about.' It felt like nothing I did was good enough. *I* was never good enough. I messed up on a project and got my ass handed to me. I ended up breaking down in tears at my desk and quit on the spot. I spent days depressed alone in my bed."

I rubbed my thumb across her cheek. My heart ached at the distraught look on her face. "Sweet thing, has Dec ever done that?"

"Well, no..."

"Do you like working for the brewery?"

"Yes, of course. I love it."

"It sounds like you have your answer, then."

She furrowed her brow. "I do?"

"You'll be awesome as the marketing director for the brewery. Declan trusts all your wacky ideas."

She frowned and crossed her arms over her chest. "My ideas aren't wacky!"

I grinned.

She slapped my arm. "You did that on purpose!"

I grinned again and brought her down for a kiss. She sighed into it, and I pulled back when I realized that cloud of sadness had come over her again. "What's wrong?"

She leaned her head into the crook of my neck. "We go home soon."

"I know."

"I kinda don't want to. I wish we could stay here in this bubble together."

"Gemma, baby..."

She looked up at me. "What?"

"I—"

She hopped off me. "I know. You can't. I get it. It's fine."

It wasn't fine. Neither of us wanted this to end, but it had to.

She hopped back into the driver's seat and drove me around the lake. She told me funny stories about all her adventures as a kid while I drew her in my sketchbook. She looked so beautiful with the wind in her hair while she manned the boat. Her eyes lit up with excitement as she told me all the ways she got in trouble as a kid.

I shaded in the lines of her hair on my drawing. I was in big trouble. The biggest kind of trouble. Because I didn't want to let her go. I didn't want to go back to Drakesville without her being my woman.

"I'm sorry," she said.

"For what?" I asked, and looked up from my sketching.

"I promised you it would only be for this week. I know on Sunday that's the end of you and me. I told you I'd be okay with that."

I frowned and ran a hand through my hair. I wasn't sure what to say to her. "Are you not okay with that now?"

She shook her head. "I know that's the deal, so we'll have to make up for it these next couple of days."

I cocked my head at her. "What are you proposing?"

She grinned. "We go back to the cabin for the rest of the day."

I smirked at her. "Oh, what for?"

She drove the boat back to the dock. "You know what for. I want to have you all to myself before dinner."

I grinned at her. "I can get behind that."

"Well, I definitely want you behind me."

I laughed. "Gemma Jensen, you dirty girl."

She smirked at me. "You know it!"

＊

"Oh, my god!" Gemma moaned as she collapsed face down onto the pillow. "Fuck me, that was so good."

I kissed her shoulder and pulled out of her. "It was good for me too, sweet thing."

She lifted a hand to show me her middle finger. I laughed and got rid of the condom. I lay back on the bed with my arms behind my head, and Gemma turned to cuddle into my arms. Her head on my shoulder and her hand tracing my tattoos felt amazing.

I stroked her hair and kissed the top of her head. "Have you had enough yet?"

She laughed into my chest. "You have wrecked my pussy, utterly and completely."

"So, yes?"

"Nope. I want you as much as possible. Who knows when I'll get laid again?"

I reached a hand down and rubbed my thumb across her plump bottom lip. She parted her lips, and I slid my thumb inside. She gave me a seductive look as she sucked on it, and I felt my dick lift in interest again. God, she made me so damn horny.

"I love when these pretty lips are wrapped around my cock."

"Mmm," she moaned and took my thumb out of her mouth. "What else do you like?"

"When you ride my beard, I think, if I die, this is the way to go. With my girl coating my beard with her cum. I like that you trust me to choke you while I fuck you into submission. And how you cry out my name when you finally come."

"I love all of that too," she purred. "I want more and more."

"You have to wait."

She pouted. "Please, Felix."

"Later, sweet thing. I need to eat first."

"Mean!" she whined.

I kissed the top of her head. "You're the one who invited your friends over."

She frowned. "Oh, right, I forgot. Let's go eat so we can get another quickie in before they get here!"

"You're a naughty girl, Gemma Jensen."

She gave me a bright smile. "Your naughty girl."

I certainly liked the sound of that, but we both knew this was temporary. She got out of bed and walked into the bathroom. I lay in bed and waited to hear the shower.

"Are you coming?" she called from the other room.

"What?"

"We're both sandy from the lake. Come take a shower with me before we eat."

I think I ran to the bathroom.

She got in first, and I followed behind her. I watched as the water flowed down her body. She ran her hands through her hair as she got it wet, and it was like something out of a fantasy. I was naked in the shower with Gemma Jensen, and she was teasing me as she touched herself.

My dick, which I thought needed some time to recover, thickened against my leg. Gemma looked down at it and licked her lips.

"Gemma," I warned, but then she kneeled in front of me.

The water slid down her hair and I wrapped it around

my hand. Those big blue eyes looked up at me as if asking for permission. As if she needed that to suck my dick.

She kissed my thighs until she got to my shaft. She held it loosely in her hand while licking me from root to tip.

"Sweet thing," I growled.

"What?' she asked innocently.

"Wrap those pretty lips around my cock right now."

"Or what?" she dared.

I gripped her hair tighter. "I'm gonna shove it down your throat and face fuck you."

She gave me that pouty look again.

"Oh you, brat, you want that, huh?"

She nodded.

"No, put it in your mouth yourself."

I had to put a hand on the tile wall to steady myself when she did. Gemma slid my dick into her mouth, taking me as far back as she could. Instinctively, I pumped my hips, and she let me. I wasn't sure I could come again, but she didn't care. It was so hot how much she enjoyed going down on me.

She had a hand between her legs and rubbed her clit while she sucked me off. I tipped back my head in pleasure and let the water roll down my body. Shower head was awesome.

She moaned around my cock, and I knew she was close.

"There you go, sweet thing. Moan around my cock while you suck me off."

She nodded and rolled her hips into her hand.

"You think about me when you get yourself off?" I asked.

She nodded again and worked her fingers faster against her clit.

"Yeah, you do. You dream about choking on my dick, huh?"

She moaned around the dick in her mouth while she came all over her hand. That did it for me. I watched my dick sliding in and out of her mouth for a couple more seconds until I groaned and came down her throat. She sucked it down like the good little brat she was, and then she stood up and faced the showerhead.

I wrapped my hand around her throat from behind and held her against my chest. "You're a little brat."

She giggled and pressed back into me. "I didn't see you complaining while I lapped up all your cum."

I gave her ass a little slap. "You got off on it, too. You couldn't help yourself when you had my dick in your mouth, huh? You had to touch yourself while you took it down your throat."

She leaned her ass back against me and rubbed herself on me. "Sucking your dick makes me horny."

I tightened my grip around her throat. "Such a dirty girl. What am I gonna do with you, huh?"

"Fuck me?" she offered.

"Later, little brats have to wait," I said and released my hold on her.

She whimpered but then started washing her hair. She handed the shampoo off to me and ran it through my hair. The water had turned lukewarm by now, but we didn't care. At least I didn't. Not after what she just did. Such a fucking brat, but I loved that about her. Loved that she challenged me in bed.

She put body wash into her hands and rubbed them together, then ran her hands down my tattooed arms and washed me. I did the same for her, making her laugh when I played with her tits for too long. We washed the rest of our bodies quickly once the shower got ice cold.

I grabbed my towel when I stepped out of the shower and dried off before wrapping it around my waist. I grabbed a towel for Gemma and dried her off when she stepped out after me. She looked so cute, wrapped in that big fluffy towel.

I got dressed but walked back into the bathroom to find her inspecting her hair.

I wrapped my arms around her behind and put my head on her shoulder. She smiled at me through the reflection in the mirror. "Looks like you didn't need to eat," she said.

I squeezed her ass. "You're such a brat. Never doing what you're told."

"You love it," she teased, but then she frowned as she looked at her hair.

"What's wrong?"

She waved me off. "Oh, nothing. I just need to re-dye my hair. My roots are atrocious. I'll do it when I get home because the lake water is terrible on my hair."

I twirled a strand of pink around my finger. "I love your pink hair. It suits you."

She beamed.

"I can't picture you without it. You wouldn't be you."

I tilted her head toward me and kissed her. I pretended my heart wasn't imagining what it would be like to have these small moments with her every day. My logical brain had to keep telling it to be quiet.

CHAPTER NINETEEN

GEMMA

"*Y*ou want help with dinner?" Felix asked.

I waved him off. "I'm just putting a pizza in the oven. Go do whatever work you want to do."

He smiled at me. After we got out of the shower, I noticed he had that look in his eye, like he was plotting something. He grabbed his paint set and easel with the unfinished painting. "I want to go down to the dock and finish this."

"Babe, go!" I said, and I wanted to stop myself from calling him that. He wasn't my boyfriend. Come Sunday, we would go back to barely being friends. I shouldn't call him that. Even though he got a shy little smile on his face when I did.

He kissed my cheek and walked out of the cabin.

I went into the fridge and grabbed a 611 Ale. I popped the top off with the bottle opener on the fridge. I took a sip and set the beer on the counter again, then opened the freezer, took out the frozen pizza, and put it in the oven.

I was exhausted from taking Felix out on the boat today and from the marathon sex afterward. We were trying to squeeze every moment out of the rest of our vacation together. In two days, this would be over, but I didn't want it to be. I just didn't think I could convince him otherwise.

I sat on the couch in the living room and sipped my beer while I spied Felix out on the dock with his painting. He looked in the zone, and I didn't want to bother him. He seemed so sure of his place in the world, and I liked how invested he got into making me a new logo for my shop.

I pulled out my phone and tried to see if I could get on the internet. I searched his name but couldn't find anything. I found his website linked in the bio on his social media accounts. His website was amazingly put together, which wasn't a surprise since Felix put a lot of care into his work. All the stuff he did for the Brewery was in his portfolio, but he also had logos he had done for different businesses, and even some sports teams. He was fantastic at this, and I felt confident he'd give me a logo that exuded my essence.

I set my phone down and forced myself to think about the marketing job. That had been the whole point of coming up here this week. I loved working at the brewery, but it was a dead-end job. It wasn't like I could become 'head bartender.' The only place to grow was to become the house manager, and I wasn't sure I wanted that either. I loved helping come up with the beer names and new ways to get our name out there.

Maybe I *should* take the position.

I went back into the kitchen and found the shopping list notepad in the junk drawer. I found a pen and sat at the kitchen table as I started a pros and cons list for taking the job.

PRO: *Career growth, be my own boss, have control over marketing ideas, career path if I ever leave the brewery, bigger salary.*

CON: *Failing, No longer interacting with customers.*

The pros outweighed the cons by a lot. My biggest reason for not wanting the job was my fear of failure. My fear of having the same thing happen as when I worked that soul-crushing corporate job. But Felix was right. Declan never treated me the way my old boss had.

When I stared back at my words, I realized I finally had my answer. But it didn't mean I wasn't still scared about my future.

My timer beeped, and I went to check on the pizza. I took it out of the oven and let it cool on the stove. I walked out onto the porch, but I felt bad bothering Felix when he looked so engrossed in his work.

"Hey!" I called out to him. He turned around, and I had to lift my hand above my eyes to spy on him. "Dinner's ready!"

He held up a finger and went back to painting.

I gave him five minutes, and when he still didn't come in, I piled slices of pizza on a plate and held our beers in my other hand. I walked down the wooden steps to the dock. Felix was still too focused on his painting of the lake view to notice me. He had perfectly captured all the colors of the sky at this time of day. It was amazing what his hands could spit out on the canvas.

He turned at the sound of my footsteps and frowned. "Shit, sorry. I got too in the zone."

He took a slice of pizza from me as he examined his

work. I handed him the beer, and he gave me a quick kiss on the cheek.

I sat down on the dock, took a bite of my pizza, then took off my shoes and put my feet into the water. I loved being down here by the dock, especially as the sun was going down.

"What do you think?" Felix asked.

I turned to him and looked at his painting. "It's beautiful. Your art's amazing."

His chest puffed out in pride, and he joined me in sitting on the dock. We drank our beer and ate our pizza quietly as the sun went down in front of us.

"I think I'm gonna take the job," I said after a few minutes of comfortable silence.

"Really?" Felix asked. "Sweet thing, that's great. You'll do amazing at it."

I cocked my head at him. "You started that whole 'sweet thing' to annoy me, didn't you?"

He grinned. "Yeah, but you like it, don't you?"

I nodded. I did. I shouldn't have. It was so cheesy, but when he said it and looked at me like I was the only woman in the entire universe, it made my heart sing.

He put an arm around me, and I leaned my head on his shoulder. "It's because you're such a sweet little thing."

I pulled back and gave him an annoyed look. "I'm not a little thing!"

He laughed and rubbed his beard. "No, you're a tall woman, but I still tower over you, and you fit so perfectly beside me."

I smiled at him and leaned against his shoulder again. I wanted to remember this vacation forever. Remember the time I spent with him this week. Even if, come Sunday, things went back to the way they used to be. But my heart would be broken again. I had to amp myself up for that.

He lifted my hand up and kissed the bi pride tattoo on the back of my wrist. "I'm glad you're taking the job. You've never struck me as a woman afraid of anything. You jump two feet into anything you do."

I shrugged. "I don't want Declan to think he made a mistake. I know everyone thinks I'm flaky and unreliable. Sometimes that's true, but I don't want to prove that."

He shook his head. "You never seemed flaky to me. You get excited about all the things, and it's so cute how you jump up and down when there's something you want to do."

I laughed. "You just like watching my tits bounce!"

He gave me a sly smile. "Well...that too. But it's your energy, your passion for what you do. You're gonna be the most amazing marketing director for the brewery."

"Thank you," I muttered. I finished my pizza and drained my beer. "I'm gonna get the fire going."

"I'll help."

I waved him off. "Finish your painting."

He looked back at his canvas. "I think it's done. You really like it?"

I nodded. "It's gorgeous. You really captured what it's like here. When I look at it, it reminds me of how much I love coming here. It's like all my cares are forgotten for a few days."

He picked up his paint palette. "I need to make a few minor touch-ups."

I gave him a quick kiss. "Finish it, babe. I'll start getting the fire going."

His hand lingered on my hip, and it looked like he

wanted to say something else, but then he turned back around and inspected his painting again.

I left him be and went back inside to get wood from the rack. The first night here, when I made that fire and tried to make nice with Felix, I had chopped a bunch of extra wood so we could do more fires. The last one had ended prematurely, but since Harper and Keisha were coming over, that wasn't happening tonight.

I grabbed the logs and matches and went back outside. I laid the big pieces on the ground while I collected the tinder, which I arranged in the center of the fire, and lit a match. I tossed that into the fire pit and watched the fire build. As the light of the fire died down, I added more tinder and blew at the base.

"There's my mountain woman," Felix teased as he walked his painting and supplies back into the house.

I shook my head at him while I stood and watched the fire. I put one of the bigger pieces into the fire and watched it build. I sat back in one of the chairs and rubbed my hands down my arms. The sun had set, and it was getting darker out. I needed to change into warmer clothes for the cooler mountain air. Felix came back outside wearing a long-sleeved flannel and jeans. He held two plates of pizza for both of us.

I gave him a bemused look.

"I'm still hungry, and you only had one slice," he said.

"In a minute, I need to change."

I went back inside and into the bedroom where I had dropped my clothes. I hadn't slept in the bedroom I normally stayed in since the night of the thunderstorm. I was so scared that night. I was grateful Felix had been there to comfort me in more ways than one.

I changed and went back outside. Felix was staring into

the fire like he had a lot on his mind. I wondered what he was thinking about. If he was also struggling with the fact that we had to go back to the way things were before in a couple of days. I wanted so badly to know if he wanted me like I wanted him. My hopeful little heart wanted to believe he was holding back because he felt like he had to.

I sat down next to him and took my pizza from him. I chewed it while I watched the fire crackle to life in front of us. Felix put a hand on my thigh as we sat together for a few minutes in silence.

"Can I ask you something?" he asked after a few more minutes had passed.

"Hmm?"

"What's your history with Harper?"

I laughed. "Oh. That. I was wondering when you would ask."

He ran a hand across his beard. "Let me guess...first love?"

I nodded. "Bingo."

"What happened?"

"The usual. She wasn't ready to be out. She told me we couldn't hang out anymore because she wasn't 'supposed to like women.' I came out to my dad the next summer. We reconnected this week. I haven't seen her in years."

He lifted an eyebrow in surprise. "You seemed so close."

I shook my head. "That's the lake. You come up here, and you haven't seen people for years, but the week you're here, it's like you've never left. We spent a lot of summers hanging out and chasing boys. I chased girls too."

"You hoe," he teased.

I swatted at his thigh. "Don't slut shame me!"

"Never, sweet thing."

A car drove up to the cabin, and we both turned to see

Keisha and Harper jump out. I waved a hand at them. "Come on over. I got the fire going!"

They walked over to us and took seats opposite us across the ring of the fire.

Felix jumped up. "Beers?"

They both nodded.

"What do you like?" he asked.

"What do you have?" Keisha asked.

Harper put her hands under her chin. "Yeah, sell us on them."

Felix waved to me. "Come on, marketing director, do your thing."

"You're taking the job?" Harper asked.

I nodded. "I think so. I'm still thinking about it."

"Well, sell those beers to us, girl!" Keisha said.

"Okay, we've got four selections for you tonight. We have 611 Ale, that's a malty yet crisp pale ale. That's my favorite. Then we got Area 267, that's your typical hoppy IPA. If you're looking for a more summer-time beer, we got Radle My Cage. That's a lemon radler. Traditionally, it's a beer and lemonade split, but we brew ours with real lemons to give it that citrus taste and be a more traditional beer. Last is our newest beer, Mac Daddy. It's a traditional hefeweizen with a fruity aroma and clove taste," I sputtered off.

Felix grinned. "See, she's good at this."

"So are you!" I exclaimed. "We do this at the brewery when people don't know what they want. It's second nature."

"I know what you want, sweet thing," Felix said, but he looked at the other women. "What about you two?"

"Ooh, Radler sounds good," Keisha said.

"I'll take Mac Daddy," Harper said and laughed. "Mostly because I love the name."

"You'll die when you see the artwork he did," I told them.

Felix went inside to go get the beers. I should have told him to bring out the s'mores supplies. I hadn't gotten that far yet.

I got up to put another log on the fire and made sure it kept going.

"You should take the job, Gem," Harper said.

I nodded. "I made a pro and con list. I think I might. I was just scared. Still am."

"Can't fail if you don't try," Keisha said.

I nodded. True, but that was what I was afraid of.

Felix came back with our beers and handed them out. We clinked beer bottles, and Harper laughed hysterically. "Oh, my god! This artwork's amazing!"

Felix smiled.

"It's perfect!" I agreed.

"Is that supposed to be your niece?" Keisha asked.

I nodded. "Yup. She's the cutest, and Nolan's so cute with her. He melts for her."

"And your sister. They have him wrapped around their fingers," Felix said.

I laughed. "That too. Nolan's a grump, but not with my sister. She's his light or some shit."

Harper laughed. "She needs to bring the baby up to the cabin!"

"She will," I reassured her. "She literally had her a couple of weeks ago."

"I just want to smell that new baby smell!"

Keisha smiled and reached out to hold her wife's hand. "Excuse her, Harper has baby fever."

"Is that catching? Because I don't want it," I said and shivered.

"You don't want kids?" Harper asked, her mouth agape.

I shook my head. "Nah. I like to hand them back."

Keisha looked at Felix. "What about you, Felix? Kids?"

He shook his head. "Nah. I've been raising my little sister since I was fourteen. I'm good." He paused for a second. "That makes me sound like a dick. I love my little sister. I'd do anything for her. She's my world, but I lost a lot of myself in being the parent mine couldn't be. Raising a kid's hard, and I don't think I want to do it again."

Keisha looked curiously at the two of us. "Interesting."

I jumped up to deflect from the conversation. "Let me grab the s'mores stuff, and we can roast marshmallows."

I skipped back into the house before any of them could say anything else.

It was not lost on me that Felix and I were on the same page about kids. I had to tell my heart to shut the fuck up and forget about that.

CHAPTER TWENTY

FELIX

*T*he fire had started to die down, but I didn't care because, at some point in the night, Gemma ended up in my lap. I held her hip in my hand as she and Harper laughed and reminisced about past summers when they were teens.

It was fun to see Gemma in her element. My heart was yelling at me to listen to it, to let her inside, and I was drunk enough to consider it. I forgot my responsibilities when the pink-haired woman looked at me like I hung all the stars in the night sky for her.

"It's really beautiful at night in the woods," Keisha said.

I stared at Gemma's profile while she laughed in my lap. "Yeah, it is," I agreed.

"Hey, who did that painting in the living room?" Harper asked.

Gemma beamed. "Isn't it amazing? That's all Felix. I didn't even know he painted and shit when I got here."

I laughed. "Yes, Gemma, because that's exactly what it's like. Paint and shit."

She stuck her tongue out at me, but I caught her in a quick kiss.

She ended it quickly, probably because we would haven't stopped if her friends weren't here. We were both a little tipsy already. Keisha stopped drinking an hour ago, even though Gemma offered to let them stay in one of the other rooms. They didn't want to impose. I was sure they were just being polite and could smell the pheromones coming off us.

"Do you have a website?" Harper asked. "I'd love to get one for the shop."

"He does!" Gemma exclaimed.

"You know about my website?" I asked. My website wasn't under my full name, just simply Jameson Designs.

Gemma nodded. "Babe, I social media stalked you to find it. You gotta put that everywhere!"

"Why's that?" I asked.

"So we can get you more work. You're so talented. I can't wait to see what you do with my logo. I'm totally paying you, you know."

I shook my head. "No, sweet thing. I'm doing that for you because I want to."

She shook her head. "Fe, don't. You deserve to be paid for your work."

"You've already paid me in kisses."

All three of the women laughed at that.

"So cute!" Harper squealed.

Keisha looked at Harper and then at her watch. "We should get going."

"No!" Gemma cried.

Harper laughed. "Gemma, it's late. We gotta get home."

I let go of Gemma's hip, and she got up off my lap to say goodbye to her friends. I stood up too and watched with a smile as she gave Harper a big hug. I couldn't hear what they were saying to each other, but Harper eyed me, so it had to be about me. Keisha walked over to me and shook my hand.

"It was good to meet you, Felix," she said.

"Likewise."

She gave me a quick hug. "Be good to Gemma."

I raised my eyebrow.

Keisha raised her own brow back at me, but didn't explain herself. Gemma hugged her too, and then I got a hug goodbye from Harper.

"Take a chance on her," Harper whispered in my ear. "I was scared once too and missed my opportunity."

I wanted to ask her what she meant, but she pulled away. I watched silently as Keisha and Harper waved to us and walked to their car. Gemma stood beside me, pressing herself into my side while we watched their car drive away.

Gemma sighed.

"What's wrong?" I asked.

She shrugged. "Nothing. Just end of vacation blues."

"We have one more day. We'll make it count," I told her. "Do you want to head to bed?"

She shook her head. "Let's wait for the fire to burn out."

I went back to my seat and patted my lap. "I got your seat right here."

She smiled and sat down on my lap again. She rubbed her thumb across my beard. "I like this seat better."

I waggled my eyebrows at her. "Oh yeah? You want to sit on your throne upstairs for a bit?"

She laughed. "Not yet. I want to enjoy the last fire of vacation."

"We can have another one tomorrow night," I offered.

She shook her head. "Nah. Tonight being the last one feels right. I think I'm gonna want to chill and go to bed early tomorrow."

She leaned her head on my shoulder, and we sat together for a little while longer, watching the last embers of the fire die down. We were both thinking hard, but this time, Gemma didn't thrust a stone at me to channel all my energy into. This time, she was feeling the weight of our fling ending. We had one more day together, and I was going to make it count.

Eventually, the fire died out, and Gemma went to douse it completely. I cleaned up while she took care of the fire. I was doing the dishes at the sink when she surprised me by wrapping her arms around my waist from behind and kissing my neck.

"Hey, you," I said as I turned in her arms. I brushed her hair out of her face and kissed her forehead. "You ready for bed?"

She nodded and yawned.

We trudged up the steps together and got ready for bed. I crawled into bed first, and Gemma came in after me. She laid her head on my chest and I stroked her hair. I didn't know how I was going to manage sleeping without her by my side. I had been so afraid of breaking her heart that I never thought of the possibility of breaking my own. There was something inside me screaming that she was worth it, that I could make it work for us, but my brain knew what happened whenever I tried to have something for myself.

"You wanna go to sleep?" I asked.

We were lying in bed with all the lights on, not saying a word to each other, but not sleeping, either.

"I wore myself out with all the sex this afternoon," she admitted with a sleepy smile.

I kissed her temple. "You were insatiable!"

She giggled. "I can't help it. You make me so horny. I want to squeeze all the pleasure out of you."

I frowned. "Gross."

She looked up at me and wrinkled her nose. "Gross?"

I grinned. "Yeah, it sounds like you want to milk me dry of all my jizz."

She laughed. "That's not what I meant!"

I cocked my head at her in response.

"FELIX! It's not!" She laughed.

I laughed and kissed the back of her hand. "I know, but that's how it sounded."

"Men," she muttered.

"So, last day tomorrow, what's the plan?"

She laid her head back down on my chest and didn't say anything for several minutes. I stroked her hair while we cuddled together.

A part of me wanted this with her every night. This week with her had been amazing, and I didn't want it to end. Maybe it was too soon to feel this way about her, but there was something about Gemma that made me feel like I could have it all. Because she was worth it.

"Felix?" she asked.

I looked down at her, and she gave me a worried look. "Hmm?"

"Did you hear a word I just said?"

"Sorry. I got into my own head."

"I want to get some of the cleaning done tomorrow, so we're not rushing around on Sunday. Then maybe do a hike. There are great walking trails around the lake. Or we can go to the nature preserve."

"Let's go out to dinner," I said.

"We don't have to."

"Let me rephrase that. Let me take you out to dinner."

She gave me a curious look. "Why?"

"Let me take you out on that date I promised you."

She shook her head. "That's okay."

"But, I want to."

Her smile lit up her entire face. "Okay."

"I owe you that."

"Okay, but we don't have to go anywhere fancy. You know I'm good for pizza and beer."

I laughed. "I know, but I want our last night together to be special."

"Me too."

I pressed my lips against hers in a soft kiss. She let me take the lead as I savored the feeling of her lips on mine. Kissing Gemma was like coming in from out of the cold. I didn't want to stop kissing her or think about how lonely I'd be without her after this week.

I pulled away, and she got up to turn off all the lights. She slid back into bed and curled onto her side. I wrapped an arm around her waist and held her against my chest. We fell asleep wrapped in each other's arms.

As I was drifting off to sleep, the last thing on my mind was that the Poconos had put a spell on me, and I didn't want it to be broken come Sunday.

CHAPTER TWENTY-ONE

GEMMA

I hated the last day of vacation. Which was why I woke up early and slithered out of bed, hoping I didn't wake Felix. He looked so peaceful sleeping beside me, but I wanted to do ALL the things before I had to go back to Drakesville tomorrow.

I went into the bedroom I had previously been sleeping in to change my clothes. The sun had just about risen, and I wanted to get out on the lake. Then I'd make a big breakfast before we went out on our hike. I wasn't a baker like my sister, but I made a mean French toast.

I tip-toed down the wooden steps of the cabin, careful not to step on the creaky one at the bottom. I slipped out the back door and went into the garage. I found the kayak and paddle and walked them down to the shoreline. I put on my life vest and got in, pushing off from the shore and putting my paddle in the water.

I closed my eyes and let the sun shine down on me. Being out on the lake this early in the morning always made me feel calm. I slid my paddle into the water and took in the surrounding scenery. The lake was beautiful, especially at this time of day as the water shimmered beneath the sun. As I paddled across the lake, my thoughts turned to dread about leaving tomorrow.

This week with Felix had been amazing, but it was a dream. Up here, we were in our own romantic bubble, but tomorrow we'd go our separate ways and never speak of this again. That was why it made little sense when he said he wanted to take me out to dinner tonight. I didn't understand why he wanted it to be a makeup date from when he stood me up if all of this was about to be over. We'd probably have amazing goodbye sex tonight, but that's all it would be—a goodbye.

I had thought this week would be hell. That we'd have bickered all week, and I'd have driven home way sooner than I planned. But in a few short days, I fell for him. I fell for him hard.

If I was honest with myself, it was probably when he told me about his dad and sister. He sacrificed his own happiness for his sister's, which made my heart thrum for him. He wasn't the asshole he made me believe he was. He pushed me away because he thought we didn't have a future.

And yet, yesterday, it felt like he looked at me like he was wondering if it was possible. If he could take a chance on me. Last night in bed, when he zoned out, I wanted so badly to know what he was thinking. I wanted to open up that brain of his and pick out what he focused on.

The other part of me wondered if he had been tired, and I just saw what I wanted to see. Felix was a good man, and I understood why he and Nolan got along so well. Declan said after their parents died, Nolan sacrificed his whole life to make sure food was on the table. Just like Felix did for his sister. It was admirable, and I'd admit it was one of the reasons I'd fallen for him. But he made it clear we couldn't have anything more. So loving him wasn't an option. It would only lead to heartbreak.

I paddled myself back to shore and willed the dark thoughts to the back of my mind. I'd deal with those thoughts tomorrow after I got home. I'd cry and eat ice cream, watching old hockey games to cheer myself up. But today, I'd spend one last day in Felix's arms.

I spied a figure on the dock as I paddled the kayak closer. I glanced at my watch and realized I had been out on the lake much longer than I thought. As I got closer, Felix's image materialized. He stood on the dock with two mugs of coffee, waiting for me.

Oh, a man who waited for you with coffee was definitely a keeper and sexy as all hell. Too bad keeping this one was never an option.

I paddled to shore and got out of the kayak on the grassy side next to the dock. I rested the paddle against a tree and walked over to Felix. He gave me a big smile. "You could have woken me up."

He handed me the steaming cup of coffee, and I took a sip. My eyes lit up when my tastebuds realized he remembered how I took it. "I didn't want to wake you," I explained.

He sipped his black coffee and raised that pierced eyebrow of his. "Mmmhmm."

"Fine," I sighed. "I wanted to do all the things, and you weren't waking up."

A smile tugged at the corner of his mouth.

I handed him the mug back. "Give me a sec. I have to put the kayak away, and then I'll make breakfast."

"You're making me breakfast?" he teased.

"Breakfast is my specialty. I know you loved my pancakes."

He gave me an exasperated look. "Those were from a box, Gem."

I opened my mouth in shock and fake gasped. "Who told you?"

He laughed. "The pantry."

I shrugged and lifted the kayak into my arms. I liked that he didn't tell me he'd get it for me because he knew I could handle it.

I walked back over to the garage and hung the kayak up to dry. I undid my life vest and hung that up too, then went back into the cabin. Felix was already at the counter, cracking eggs into a mixing bowl. He left my coffee at the table for me.

I picked up my coffee and took a sip, then walked over to him. He gave me a smile as he whisked the eggs, but I distracted him with a quick kiss.

"Morning," I breathed when our lips parted from each other.

"Morning, sweet thing. I was gonna make us French toast."

I laughed. "That's what I was gonna make you!"

He laughed. "It's my favorite."

"Mine too!"

He smiled. "Then, let's make it together."

I took another sip of my coffee and set it back down. I took a platter out of the cabinet and set it down on the counter. I grabbed the bread from the table and piled slices onto the platter while Felix worked on the egg mixture.

Once he scrambled everything, he gave that to me to dip the bread in and cook while he started cutting up fruit.

"You want bacon, too?" I asked.

"Oh, yeah, that would be great."

I pulled another pan out, set it on the stove, and got the bacon out of the fridge. I started the bacon first and got it going before I began the French toast. I dipped slices into the egg mixture and cooked them quickly. Felix set out the bowl of fruit and then took over with the bacon.

In no time, we had our breakfast ready, and I had to admit, something about us working together in the kitchen side-by-side made my heart think about how good we were together. How well we fit together. I told my heart to be quiet.

We ate in comfortable silence, eating our food and sipping our coffee. It was a pleasant morning of us enjoying each other's company.

"What's the grand plan?" Felix asked as he took our empty plates into the sink and began cleaning up.

"Hike around the lake?" I offered.

He nodded. "Okay, let's do it. Then what?"

I shrugged. "Get cleaning done and relax before dinner. Where are you taking me?"

"Somewhere nice," he said with a sly smile.

I squinted at him. "Like where?"

He sighed. "Can't you just let it be a surprise?"

"Should I dress nice?" I asked.

He thought about it for a moment. "Yeah, that dress you wore the other night would be fine."

I squinted at him. Men didn't really understand the need for us to know. I knew that dress looked good on me, but I didn't know if it was fancy enough.

"Let me get dressed so we can go on that hike," he said.

"Yay!"

I ignored the laughter that rumbled from him as he

walked away. I checked my phone while I waited for him. I was dressed and ready to go, and he was taking his sweet time. I saw another text from Declan. I'd tell him in person the good news. I was still nervous about taking the job, but after thinking about it a lot, I would be foolish not to take it.

A few minutes later, Felix came down the steps, and we left the cabin. We walked down to the dock and along the lake. I adjusted the hat on my head as the sun beat down on us. Felix's hand swung near mine, and he surprised me by lacing our fingers together.

I turned to him and gave him a smile.

He winked at me and brought my hand up to his mouth and kissed the back of it. I loved when he did it. It was such a sweet gesture, and it made me feel all giddy inside.

"I like it up here," he said after a few minutes.

"Me too. It's my favorite place!" I exclaimed.

He smiled. "It shows. You're all go-go-go. I'm surprised taking this leisurely stroll isn't too boring for you."

I shook my head and swung our linked hands. "Nah. It's nice being with you. This week has been amazing."

"Mmmhmm."

I didn't press him on that noncommittal noise as we continued our walk. I was considering driving up to the nature preserve, but it felt like he wanted to stay put. I had to do some cleaning in the cabin today, anyway.

After we walked along the lake some more, Felix turned me around.

"Hey!" I yelled.

He put his arms around my waist from behind and kissed my neck. "Let's head back before you make me walk around the entire lake."

I laughed. "We could do that!"

He walked beside me, and we headed back in the

cabin's direction. I didn't mind the silence between us, since it wasn't tension-filled anymore. We were comfortable enough that we just wanted to be present with each other.

When we got back to the cabin, Felix tackled the dishes while I started a load of wash. Upstairs in the bedroom, I grabbed a handful of his clothes but paused when I saw his sketchbook lying open on the bed.

I sat on the bed and studied the image drawn in dark pencil. It was me. Felix was drawing me. In the sketch, I had my eyes closed, like I was asleep. I turned the page and found another similar sketch, but this time I was chopping wood for the fire. The next one, I had my eyes closed again, but I was sitting on the dock with my feet in the water. Felix kept drawing me in different scenarios in his sketchbook, and I didn't know why.

I turned the page, and the next drawing was of the two of us. Felix had his arms around my waist from behind, and he was kissing my temple while we stood on the dock, looking out at the water. We looked so deeply and desperately in love.

Was I only seeing what I wanted to see? Or was Felix trying to tell me something with his drawings? When I looked at all these images, all I felt was love, like maybe he was fooling himself too.

"Sweet thing!" Felix called from downstairs.

I jumped at the prospect of getting caught snooping. He might have left his sketchbook open, but I wasn't supposed to see this. His drawings were the window to his soul, and he didn't want to share his feelings with me. At least not yet. But maybe I could convince him we were good together. Maybe this was a sign from the universe that he didn't want to let me go either.

"Gemma!" Felix yelled again. "Did you forget about the wash?"

I snapped out of it as I yelled back down to him. "Coming!"

I piled his clothes back into my arms and went downstairs. I dumped all the clothes into the washing machine and started it up.

"Did you throw it all in?" he asked from his seat on the couch. He was chewing on his lip as he stared at something on his computer screen.

"Yeah?"

"Gemma, you gotta separate the wash."

I shrugged. "It's fine! I put it all on cold."

He shook his head in disbelief.

I flopped down on the couch beside him, but he moved his laptop when I tried to sneak a peek. I pouted, but he waggled a finger in my face. "No, you can't see it yet."

"Please," I begged and really turned on the adorable pout.

"Nope, don't even try it, you brat. You'll see it when it's done."

"But I want to see it now."

He placed a hand on my thigh and squeezed. "Patience, sweet thing. You'll see it soon enough."

We both knew we weren't just talking about the logo he was designing for me.

I stood up. "I'm gonna go for a swim in the lake while you're working."

He shut his laptop. "I'll join you."

I skipped up the stairs to go put on my bathing suit. Having our own dock definitely had its perks.

CHAPTER TWENTY-TWO

FELIX

"*P*lease," Gemma begged, and gave me that pouty look again.

I shook my head and rubbed my towel over it. After our swim in the lake, we put our clothes in the dryer and got a shower. We might have gotten sidetracked with a quickie when we got upstairs, though.

"Nope, not telling," I said as I dried off.

She dropped her towel, showing off her long and athletic body, but I knew that trick, and it wouldn't work on me.

I gave her a quick kiss. "Nope. Get dressed, so we don't miss our reservation."

She knitted her eyebrows together. "Reservation? Oh, Felix, you know I don't need fancy."

I cupped her face and gave her a gentle kiss. "Let me."

"You need to tell me. What if I'm not dressed well enough?"

"You're fine," I said and walked into the bedroom.

I wasn't taking her to a place that was so fancy I needed to wear a suit and tie. Last night, Harper told us about the farm-to-table restaurant at the local inn Keisha took her to on their first date. It sounded amazing, and I knew Gemma would like it. I checked it out online earlier when Gemma had been out in the kayak. It was in a cool craftsman-style lodge, and the menu looked interesting. They also had a massive beer list, which Gemma would love.

I owed her a good date after I messed up our first one.

I started putting my clothes on while Gemma stood in the bathroom doorway, naked and rubbing her towel over her head. I put on my nice pair of jeans and a black button-down shirt.

Gemma cocked her head at me curiously. "So not too fancy?"

I shook my head. "No. The dress you wore the other day's fine."

"Okay...so not too fancy, but you still won't tell me."

"Surprise," I teased.

"Mean!"

"Get your sweet ass ready."

She cocked an eyebrow at me. "Or what?"

I mirrored her expression. "You know what."

"Will you put me over your knee and spank me like the brat I am?"

"Maybe..."

"Or choke me a little harder?"

I rubbed a hand across my beard. "Both, if you don't get your ass in gear."

She laughed. "Okay, okay!"

Gemma thought for a moment and then pulled out a long white dress with sunflowers on it. It was casual yet still made her look like the most gorgeous woman in the room. I watched her dress as I combed my hair and replaced my eyebrow piercing with a black gauge that matched my shirt.

"Did that hurt?" Gemma asked.

I shook my head. "Not much. Like a pinch and then some pressure."

"What about the tongue one?" she asked.

"Nah. Nothing hurts as much as a Prince Albert."

She gave me a confused look. "You don't have a PA."

I shuddered. "Nope. Thought about it, though. A buddy of mine got one, and it looked painful."

"Why get that?" she asked and brushed out her hair.

"It makes sex better for some people, but others say it sucks, so I didn't want to take the risk."

"For the record, I'm not sure I'd like that, but I love your tongue ring."

I smirked. "That's because it vibrates."

"Even your normal gauge feels nice."

Hmm. I thought about that while Gemma went into the bathroom to blow dry her hair and do her makeup. I sat on the bed and pulled out my sketchbook. I had been drawing nothing but Gemma since we got here. I stared down at the last sketch of the two of us, and it made my heart voice its opinion again.

I shut my sketchbook, hoping to silence my thoughts, got up from the bed, and brushed myself off so there wasn't any lint on my jeans. I walked over to the bathroom and leaned against the doorway while I watched Gemma get ready. She wore a long and flowy dress, but it left her shoulders bare. She was tanned from the time spent in the sun this week. Her hair had turned a pale pink as the color faded, but she was the most beautiful creature I had ever seen.

"I'm almost done," she said, putting her lipstick on.

I was going to enjoy watching that color spread across my dick later.

She gave me a warning look.

"What?"

She raised an eyebrow. "Babe, stop giving me the horny face."

"What?"

"Can you at least wait for dinner?"

I laughed. "Yeah, sweet thing, I can wait until after dinner. You ready?"

She nodded and threw her makeup back into the bag she had on the counter. She walked out of the bathroom, and we left the cabin together in my car. I put a hand on her thigh and drove us into town. It was a quick drive to the Inn.

"Oh!" she said. "You could have told me we were going to the Inn."

"I wanted it to be a surprise. Harper spoke so highly of it."

She put a hand on my arm. "Thank you. This was a good choice."

We got out of the car and walked into the main entrance. We found the dining room for the restaurant and didn't have to wait too long before they sat us at a table. The atmosphere was a little casual, and we might have been a bit overdressed, but none of that mattered when I looked at Gemma on the other side of the table.

Gemma scanned the long beer list. "Oh! They have one of our beers."

"Which one?" I asked. I hadn't looked at the list, just saw it was a long one, and knew Gemma would like that.

"Drakesville Lager," she said, but she continued to pore over the menu.

I grinned at that. "That's a solid one."

"True. I prefer the 611 Ale or Area 267. All of which are our core pours."

"Look at you, little marketing director," I teased.

She frowned, but before I could ask what was wrong, the server came over to take our drink orders. Gemma ordered a local craft IPA beer, while I ordered a summer shandy from one of the bigger breweries.

The server left, and I scanned the menu. "What are you thinking about?" I asked.

Gemma wrinkled her nose. "Not sure yet. The pork tenderloin looks good. What about you?"

"Honestly? I might get the tofu. It sounds good."

She scanned the menu. "Crispy Tofu and vegetables over herbed quinoa. Hmm, that sounds good too."

I stroked my beard. "Or maybe the filet mignon. They all look so good."

"I love that this is farm to table."

"I know."

"Ass!"

I reached across the table and grabbed her hand in mine. Her indignation disappeared when I rubbed my thumb across the back of her palm. The way she smiled at me set my heart into a tailspin. I didn't think I could leave tomorrow and not have her be my girl.

The moment was interrupted when our server brought over our drinks. Gemma ended up getting the pork, and I got the tofu. Sometimes I liked to eat vegetarian, and after eating so much red meat this week, I wanted something lighter tonight.

Gemma and I clinked glasses together.

"This is really nice, Felix," she said after taking a few sips of her beer.

"The beer?" I asked.

She shook her head. "No, babe, the dinner. Okay, you're definitely forgiven for standing me up because I like this better than that Italian place you were gonna take me to back home."

A smile tugged at my lips. "I thought you already said I was forgiven?"

She shrugged. "Yeah, but like for reals this time."

"Thank Harper. She was talking about this place last night."

"It's perfect. I love it."

I smiled at her and sipped my drink. I looked at her from across the table, and I knew I was in trouble. I had fallen for Gemma Jensen, and there was no way I could let her go. Not when she smiled at me like I was the only man in the universe. It made me feel like the warm sun was shining down on me.

Gemma frowned suddenly, and that alarmed me.

"What's wrong?"

She shook her head.

"Gemma, tell me what's wrong."

She shook her head. "Nothing, just end of vacation blues. And...I'm still nervous about the job."

I waved her away with my hand. "Nonsense, you're going to be amazing at it. Did you tell Declan the good news yet?"

She shook her head. "No. I want to do it in person. I'm still afraid of failing."

"Well, you won't if you don't at least try. You gotta take the leap of faith."

She played with the crystal pendant around her neck. "I suppose you're right."

Our food came a few minutes later, and I watched, amused, as Gemma moaned when she ate. I loved watching how she took pleasure in the simple things in life. I cut my tofu and took a bite.

"How's the tofu?" she asked.

"Good. You want to try?"

She nodded.

I cut off a piece for her and got some quinoa on my fork. I held it out to her, and she leaned over to take a bite of it.

"Mmm, that's good. I'm not one for tofu either. Want to try my pork?"

"Sure."

She fed me a piece of her pork tenderloin and the risotto it came with. It was all very romantic.

This was the perfect first date, and I wished I never stood her up last year. Maybe if I had explained how complicated my life was, we could have made it work. I needed to find the words to tell Gemma how I felt. If I was honest with myself, I didn't fall for her in only a few short days. I fell for her the moment I saw her bright pink hair behind the bar at the brewery. And I didn't want to imagine my life without her.

We devoured dinner and talked about Gemma's plans for the brewery. Her eyes lit up with excitement as she spoke, and it put a smile on my face. No one else was suited for the marketing director job, which was why Declan had been so hard on her to take it. He saw the best in everyone and wanted to bring it out in them. Still, he could be a pushy asshole sometimes.

After we ate, we sipped on coffee and shared a slice of cheesecake for dessert. It was the perfect ending to a perfect date and the best vacation I'd had in a long time. I didn't realize how much I needed to relax. I loved my sister, and I'd always be her keeper, but it was tough being the provider and doing it all on my own.

I paid the bill while Gemma finished up her coffee. She looked contemplative, and I wanted to know what she was thinking. I wondered if she was thinking about how she couldn't let me go, either. We had agreed to one week only, but I wanted more.

"Ready to go, sweet thing?" I asked.

She nodded.

I put a hand on the small of her back and led her out to my car. I leaned her up against the passenger side door before letting her get inside. She peered up at me in surprise with her big blue eyes. I framed her face with my hands and gave her a slow kiss with the promise of more.

"Can't wait to get you out of this dress," I whispered.

She gave me a naughty smile and ran a hand down my chest. "So what's taking you so long? Let's get out of here."

"Patience, you brat. We're doing it on my terms."

She whimpered. "Felix!"

I gave her another quick kiss. "Okay, get in the car, and let's roll."

I don't think I'd ever seen her move that quickly before.

CHAPTER TWENTY-THREE

GEMMA

*a*s soon as we got inside the cabin, he was all over me. He pressed me against the kitchen wall and kissed me like it would be the last time. And it would be. This was our last night together, and we were going to make it count.

His tongue tangled with mine and his hands roamed down my body until he hitched up the bottom of my dress. "Gemma," he hissed as his fingers came across my bare pussy.

"What?" I asked innocently.

He nipped at my neck. "Such a naughty girl. You weren't wearing panties all throughout dinner?"

I shook my head and arched my hips to reach his long fingers, but he teased me by stroking the inside of my thigh instead.

"Felix," I whined.

"So naughty. What am I gonna do with you?" he whispered huskily against my ear.

"Take me upstairs?" I offered and pulled his head back up to reach my lips again.

We kissed urgently, but he still wasn't touching me where I wanted him to. He could be such a tease when he wanted to be, but I wanted those long, thick fingers pressed inside me.

"Babe, please," I whined again.

"Fine, since you've been good," he said.

I yelped when he lifted me into his arms and took me upstairs. He put me down when we got into the bedroom. He sat at the foot of the bed and undid the buttons of his shirt. I watched hungrily as he revealed the planes of his chest and all those dark lines of the tattoos on his arms.

He gestured to my dress. "Take that off."

I did as I was told. I took off my dress and unhooked my bra. I stood naked in front of him and waited for him to tell me what to do next. I loved how demanding he could be in bed. Like when he wrapped his hands around my throat or spanked my ass. Or when he told me to take all of his dick down my throat. He knew I loved it, too. Knew I loved to be the little brat that got punished by him.

He tossed his shirt on the floor and worked his jeans down his legs. I knelt in front of him and helped him out of the rest of his clothes. I wrapped my hand around his cock and gave it a couple of pumps for good measure.

He reached down and slid his thumb across my bottom lip. "I want to see your lipstick smeared on my dick."

He bunched my hair up, and I flicked my tongue out across the head of his cock.

"Now, Gemma," he snarled and pressed my head down on his cock. "Take it all, sweet thing."

I opened my mouth wider and took him inside. It was all a part of the game. We both knew I loved when he did that. I stroked him with my hand while I moved along his shaft. I slid him inside until I hit my gag and pulled back out. I sucked on the head of his cock, and then he pushed down my throat again. I licked and sucked until I was moaning around his cock, just the way he liked it.

He loosened his grip on my hair and leaned his head back in pleasure. I loved when he let go with me.

"Love watching my dick sliding in and out of your pretty lips."

I moaned and continued to give him the pleasure he wanted.

He gripped my hair harder. "You love it, don't ya, you brat?"

I looked up at him while I took him further inside and nodded.

I slid a hand down to press against my clit while I sucked him off, but suddenly his dick wasn't in my mouth anymore, and Felix hefted me onto the bed. I made an annoyed noise in the back of my throat and looked over my shoulder at him. Felix had me over his knees with my face pressed against the mattress and his hand resting on my bare ass.

"Brat," he teased, and he gave me a quick slap on my ass.

I writhed against him as he spanked me again, harder this time.

"So bad," he teased, and the loud smack of his hand against my flesh sounded across the room.

"I'll be good," I promised.

"Liar, you like being bad. You like when I spank you and choke you while I pound into you, huh?"

I whimpered in response. Yes, to all of that.

He spun me around so I was flat on my back, and he

spread my legs wide. He slid his finger across the seam of my folds, finding me wanting and wet. His other hand reached inside his mouth to turn on his tongue ring. I hadn't even noticed he switched it out when we were getting ready for dinner.

He grinned as he dipped his head down between my thighs, and he licked me from bottom to top. The vibrations of his tongue ring made me shudder in the best way possible. He pressed me into the mattress as he ate my pussy, like he could be there all night. I arched my hips up when he wrapped his lips around my clit. He smiled up at me and focused his attention back on licking me through my first orgasm.

"Felix," I moaned and tried to press my pussy as far up into his mouth as I could.

He gently pressed me back down on the bed and continued to feast on me. I gripped his hair and felt my orgasm about to cusp. This man turned me inside out with just a couple of flicks of his tongue.

"So good," I moaned and clawed at the bedsheets. "You have no idea how good that feels. Holy fuuuuck!"

He grinned up at me but didn't stop. He didn't stop until I coated his beard in my cum and screamed out his name. Until I was nothing but a pile of mushy satisfaction. He gave me one last lick across my sensitive clit and turned off his tongue ring. I melted into the bedsheets when he let me go. My whole body felt like I was floating on a cloud.

I crooked a finger at him. "Get up here."

He got up and grabbed his dick. "Oh, you want this now?"

I nodded.

He grabbed a condom from the bedside table, took it out of its package, and slid it on. I bit my lip when I watched him slick some lube down his shaft, then he spread the excess on my pussy. Fuck, it was hot how considerate he could be in bed.

He wrapped his hand around my throat and kissed me roughly. I arched up into him when he thrust inside me. I wrapped my legs around his waist and clawed my fingernails down his back as he slid his perfect dick in and out of my pussy, slowly at first.

"More," I begged.

"More?" he asked and raised his pierced eyebrow. The hand not around my neck slid down my body, and he pressed his thumb against my clit. "Or do you want me to fuck you like the animal I am?"

"That! Give me what I want, Felix."

He grinned, and I clawed against his back when he rolled his hips and took me hard. He pumped inside me frantically as we became one with each other's bodies. I squeezed my eyes shut as the pleasure coursed through me again.

"Gemma," he sighed.

"Mmm, don't stop."

He moved faster on top of me. "You feel so good."

"Mmmhmm," I moaned. "Don't stop, don't stop, please."

"Come for me, sweet thing. Come all over my dick," he growled.

"Harder, make it hurt," I begged.

A devilish smile curled up on his lips. "I'll make it hurt, you horny little brat."

I gave him an innocent smile. "I'm your brat."

"Damn straight. This pussy's mine, huh? It's made for my cock," he growled and pressed harder and faster inside me, rocking the bed beneath me.

I whimpered and arched my hips up to meet his every thrust while he choked me the way I liked.

Our bodies rocked in unison, and the headboard slapped hard against the wood paneling of the wall. I didn't want him to stop. I wanted to be forever pinned down by this man as he fucked me into submission. With his hand around my throat and the other one pressed against my clit, I came undone beneath him. My second orgasm washed over me, and I lost myself in the pleasure of it all. I lost myself in him.

"Felix!" I screamed out and dug my fingernails deeper into his back.

He moaned, and I knew he was close too, but instead of choking me harder, he cupped my face in both hands and kissed me. He devoured me with his mouth while he came inside me.

He pressed tiny kisses down my jawline until he moved to my neck. He always kissed me gently on my neck after wrapping his hand around it in a tight embrace. It was a sweet gesture of aftercare that I would miss when he was gone. We stayed joined for a moment, neither of us wanting to sever our connection quite yet. I held him tightly, willing him to never escape from my embrace.

He didn't see the tears when he rolled off me and went into the bathroom to throw out the condom. I tried to wipe them away and squeezed my eyes shut to prevent them from falling. I didn't want Felix to see me cry because my heart didn't want to let him go. I wanted to convince him we had a chance, but I was out of time. He was firm on this being just a fling, and I couldn't expect more. I wished my heart would have listened.

The bed sunk down beside me, and when I opened my eyes, Felix gave me a look of concern. His dark brown eyes were filled with worry. A stray tear slid down my cheek, and he jumped up in alarm.

"Sweet thing, what's wrong?" he asked, pulling me into his lap. He cradled me in his embrace and held me. The way he wanted to protect me made everything worse.

I shook my head, but I couldn't look at him. I couldn't tell him my feelings had gotten in the way, and I had fallen in love with him.

He gingerly pressed a hand to my neck. "Did I hurt you?"

I looked up at him in shock. "What?"

"When I choked you."

He looked upset. If he had hurt me, I would have used my safe motion. We always talked about that, but he never strayed from my boundaries. Choking during sex could be dangerous, but I trusted him completely.

"No. No, Felix, you didn't hurt me. At least not physically."

He cupped my face and stared at me deeply. "What are you saying?"

"I don't want this to end. I don't want to drive home in tears tomorrow."

His face fell. "Gem."

I held up a hand. "It's okay. You told me the rules, but my heart disobeyed."

"Gem, I don't want this to end, either."

I stared up at him with my mouth agape. "What?"

He ran a hand through my hair. "My sister will always come before you—"

"I know!" I interrupted him. "And that's okay. You could have told me what was going on instead of being a jackass."

He grimaced. "I didn't want your pity."

I raised my eyebrow in confusion.

He sighed. "I didn't want you to know how hard my life has been. That I've picked up the pieces my mom broke when she left. My dad's not a bad guy. He's in jail for drug charges. He has a disease, but it made him a shitty father. I can't be like that for my sister. She needs me."

I pressed a hand against his chest, over his heart. "Felix, that's what I love about you. You sacrificed your whole life for that little girl. You'll give her everything you never had, and that makes me like you more."

"Maybe we can try?" he offered, but he looked unsure.

"Try?"

He shrugged. "I didn't think I had the time to give you a relationship. But if you understand that there will be times I'll cancel on you because of Skye, maybe we can do this. I don't want to go home tomorrow with a broken heart because I can't have you."

I cupped his face in both of my hands. "Felix, the thought of you leaving me tomorrow breaks my heart. I don't want this to be a vacation fling."

"You'd never be a fling. You shine too bright for that. I don't want to disappoint you."

"I understand your life's complicated. But you can have it all. Job, me, and taking care of your sister. You don't have to sacrifice your love life because of your responsibilities."

I pressed a soft kiss to his lips, and he kissed me back with all the passion he could muster, like he was showing me how much he loved me with the kiss. Neither of us said the words, but we both knew what the kiss meant. I didn't know why I bothered pretending I could be okay with only one week with him.

His lips drifted down to my neck. "Gemma," he sighed.

"Yeah?"

"Say you'll be mine, please?"

I gripped his jaw. "I'm yours and you're mine, Felix Jameson."

He laughed. "No more tears, okay?"

I nodded.

He took my hand and kissed the back of my palm. Warmth spread through me at the small gesture, especially now that this man was mine and I didn't have to give him up. He kissed the back of my wrist on my bi-pride tattoo.

"I didn't expect to find love in the Poconos," he said with a chuckle.

"Fucking Avery," we said in unison and laughed together.

I got off of him and lay on my back on the bed. I snuggled into his side, feeling happiness spread through me that tomorrow I wouldn't wake up with a broken heart.

Felix stroked my hair as we lay in bed together. We would get quiet nights like this when we got home. I wasn't sure how everything would work, but we would figure it out together.

He pressed a soft kiss to my temple. "I promise you, I won't break your heart again."

I didn't know then that it was all a lie.

CHAPTER TWENTY-FOUR

FELIX

*M*y phone jolted me awake by vibrating against the bedside table. Gemma stirred on the other side of the bed, where she lay naked after we had another couple of rounds of sex. My girl was insatiable. Warmth spread across my chest that she was my girl. I wasn't sure how I was going to manage it all, but I needed her in my life.

"Babe?" Gemma moaned sleepily. "Did you set an early alarm?"

The sound of my phone buzzing reminded me of what woke me up. I pressed a kiss to her forehead. "Go back to sleep."

She turned over and went back to sleep.

I checked my phone, and panic coursed through me when I saw my sister's name on my phone screen. I jumped out of bed and threw on my boxers before tip-toeing downstairs. I didn't want to wake Gemma while I spoke to my sister. It was odd she was calling me so early. Teenagers didn't like to be awake at six a.m.

I pressed my phone to my ear and sat on the couch. "Half pint, what's wrong?" I asked.

"Felix," my sister's pained voice came over the other line.

The panic set in immediately. "What's wrong?"

"Can you come get me?" she cried.

"Whoa, slow down. What's going on?"

"Ifelloffmybikeandbrokemylegandithurts," she rushed out in one breath that I didn't catch it all.

"Whoa. Slower, Skye."

She hiccuped, and it broke my heart that I wasn't there to hug her. "I'm in the hospital in Cape May."

"WHAT?" I screeched. The gears in my head started turning a mile a minute. My sister was alone in the hospital, and I wasn't there for her.

"I'm sorry!" she sobbed. "I didn't want to ruin your vacation."

"It's okay. What happened? You want me to come get you today? I'm a few hours away, but I'll leave right now. Tell me what happened."

I heard her hiccup some more on the other line. "I fell off my bike and broke my leg. It hurts so much. Sophia's mom wants to drive us home now, but I just want you."

"All right, half pint, I'm going to leave right away. Okay?"

"Okay..."

She sounded so defeated, and I wanted to wrap my sister up in a hug and tell her everything would be okay.

"You'll be okay, half pint. I'll be there soon. Okay?"

"Okay. Thanks, big bro."

I hung up with my sister, and all I could think about

was getting to her right away. I didn't stop to think about the woman I loved lying asleep in bed. I rushed around, packed up my stuff in a rush, and left. I didn't think to leave Gemma a note or to wake her up and tell her what was going on. My mind was on autopilot, and Skye was my primary focus.

My phone died by the time I got down to Cape May, and I thought my charger was at the bottom of my bag. I didn't have time to look for it; I was too worried about my sister. When I got to the hospital, I rushed inside until I found the Parks sitting in the waiting room. Christine stood up when she saw me. I must have looked frazzled because she put a hand on my chest to stop me.

"She's fine. It's just a broken leg."

"Just a broken leg, Christine?" I snapped at her, and my jaw ticked with anger.

"Calm down," she said and gave me the 'stern mom' look.

I thrust a hand through my hair in frustration. "I wasn't there for her."

"You are now. Go on and get her."

But I didn't have to because Skye hobbled into the waiting room using crutches. She had a blue cast on her leg, and she looked annoyed. I rushed over to help her, and she gave me a pained look.

"I want to go home," she said with a look of defeat.

I nodded. "Okay, let's get you home. Say goodbye to the Parks and thank them for all they did for you."

I watched my sister say goodbye to the Parks. Sophia hugged her tight, but my baby sister looked completely miserable, and that hurt my heart. Right now, all I wanted was to get her home and comfortable. I wasn't thinking about anything else, and in hindsight, that was bad.

I helped her into the car, and we sped off down the turnpike toward Philly. I had another two-plus-hour drive on my hands, and I wasn't looking forward to it. I didn't bother trying to find my charger. I just wanted to get Skye home.

"Are you in pain?" I asked.

She nodded. "They gave me some pain medicine after they put my leg in the cast. I have to be off my feet and on crutches for six to eight weeks. What a shitty summer vacation."

"Language!" I scolded.

"Fe-fe, you swear like a truck driver. Let me complain," she huffed and crossed her arms over her chest.

I put a hand on her arm and gave her a gentle squeeze. "You're okay, and that's what matters. I know it sucks, but you'll pull through."

My mind was racing, thinking of all the stuff I'd need for her. We'd need to set her up on the couch, so she didn't have to deal with the steps. We'd have to deal with the porch steps at our house, but we'd make it work.

My mind went to thinking about the medical bills. That wasn't something my sister needed to worry about. Luckily, I had health insurance from the brewery since I was full-time, which was rare for people in the service industry. Declan felt strongly about providing benefits to his employ-ees, and it was one reason I had been with the brewery since the beginning.

I asked Skye about her trip to distract her from the pain. I listened to her go on about her beach adventures. It was unfortunate this was how her vacation ended.

"I'm sorry to cut your vacation short," she said after a few moments of silence had passed.

"It's fine," I muttered.

But at that moment, I realized I had never said a word to Gemma this morning. I had been so worried about my sister that I wasn't thinking straight. And now I couldn't tell her what was going on because my phone was dead. I felt like such an asshole. She was probably worried sick about me. Who doesn't wake up the person they love and tell them they have a family emergency?

"Do you have your charger?" I asked my sister.

"It's in my suitcase."

"Which is where?"

Skye cringed. "In Mrs. Park's car."

I clenched my jaw in annoyance. Of course. Of fucking course. Not that I was blaming my sister. This was on me. I should have woken Gemma up. I should have told her what was going on. I warned her my sister would come first, and this was one of those times. But I should have at least given her a heads up. Maybe this was a sign from the universe that we were doomed from the start.

"Fe, what's wrong?" Skye asked.

I shook my head and focused on the miles of road outstretched before me. It was going to be a long drive back to Drakesville.

When we got home, I forgot about plugging in my phone. Instead, I carried my sister up the steps into our house and set her down on the couch in front of the TV. It was mid-afternoon, and I made us lunch as we ate on the couch together.

She got cranky after a little while, so I gave her another ibuprofen. "You think you can handle the stairs?"

She chewed on her lip and used her crutches to get off the couch. "I don't know."

"Okay," I sighed and lifted her into my arms.

"Fe-fe!" she cried. "Let me at least try."

"Maybe tomorrow. Let's get you up to bed so you can lie down."

I took my sister into her bedroom and set her down on the bed. She lay down and propped her leg up on a pillow.

"Call me if you need anything. I'm here," I said and gave her a kiss on top of her head.

"Fe-fe?" she asked in a meek voice.

"Yeah, half pint?"

"Thank you for always taking care of me."

"You're my sister. It's my job."

She chewed on her lip again, and seemed like she wanted to say something, but then she shook her head instead.

"I'm gonna lay down. It was a long day of driving."

I went into my room and finally plugged my phone into the charger, but I fell asleep as soon as my head hit the pillow. In the back of my mind, I knew there was something important I had to do, but I couldn't remember what. I was too tired to remember before I drifted off to dreamland.

CHAPTER TWENTY-FIVE

GEMMA

*W*hen I woke up the next morning, I was disappointed to find I was alone in bed. But my heart was full when I remembered that after today, I wouldn't go home alone with it being broken. I'd go back to Drakesville with a heart full of love.

Last night had been perfect. From the lovely date at the inn to the way Felix tangled me up in the sheets to our heart-to-heart afterward. I thought nothing could ruin my day. I just had to find out where that man of mine had gotten off to.

I stretched my arms above my head, and when I looked at my phone, I had a mini-panic attack because it was already noon. I wanted to be on the road by noon so it wasn't too late when I got back to town. It was odd that Felix didn't wake me. He said he set an alarm for nine, so that didn't make sense. I wasn't that hard to wake up.

I got dressed and walked downstairs, but there was no sign of him. I went out onto the porch and noticed his car was missing. My heart beat loud in my head. Why didn't he wake me up? And why was his car gone? I rushed up the steps, and that's when I noticed all his things were missing.

What the fuck?

The drawers were open like he had been in a rush to leave. To leave me. Everything he said to me had been a lie. He told me last night he wanted to try. But then why had he left so suddenly? My heart felt heavy in my chest. I checked my phone, and there was nothing from him. No call, no text, nothing.

I pressed my phone to my ear and dialed his number. It went straight to voicemail. Panic set in as I worried about where he was.

"Fe, I'm really worried. Call me back as soon as you get this. I wanted to be on the road by now. Please, babe, call me back?" I begged into the phone.

I packed up my things and waited about ten minutes to see if he would call me back. I sent a text this time.

ME: *Where are you?*

I didn't wait for a response and drove into town to the coffee shop. Harper was behind the counter again. The other night, she told us she and Keisha owned the shop. She waved at me and finished helping the customer in front of me.

Her face fell when she saw my distraught expression. "What's wrong?"

"Was Felix by earlier?" I asked.

She shook her head. "No. What's up?"

"I think he left without me."

"Oh, hun. You really fell for him, huh?"

I nodded. "Last night he said he wanted to be with me, but he was gone when I woke up. He took everything and left. I don't understand."

"You call him?"

I nodded. "It's going straight to voicemail. I'm worried, Harp."

She cringed. "I'm sorry, Gemma. He seemed like a good guy."

I bit my lip to keep the tears from falling. "He is. He was. I don't know. I gotta get back home. It was great seeing you, though."

She gave me a hug from over the counter. "It was great seeing you too! Gimme a call when you're in town again."

I walked out of the coffee shop with my head hanging low in defeat. I got back into my car and drove back to the cabin, just in case Felix came back. It was futile.

I ran inside to check I hadn't left anything, but I ended up slumping down on the bed and crying. I was worried about Felix. What if something bad had happened to him? But on the flip side, my cynical heart knew he was a liar. He made me all those promises last night, but then he left without a word. This hurt more than if he told me we didn't have a future together. Telling me what I wanted to hear and then leaving was worse. My heart felt like he had ripped it out of my chest, stomped on it, and thrown it into the lake.

I wiped the tears from my eyes, but I knew it would be a rough drive home. I should have never let my heart get big ideas when it came to Felix Jameson. This was the third time he had broken it, but ever the optimist, I thought this time would be different. I thought he loved me, too.

I locked up the cabin for the second time and got back into my car. Driving home to Drakesville with a gaping hole in my chest was the worst drive of my life. When I made a pit stop, the woman behind the counter at the rest stop handed me a pack of tissues. I probably looked like a complete wreck.

When I finally got back into town, I made every plan to go home and eat ice cream in my bed, but I turned down the street toward Avery and Nolan's house.

I parked in their driveway and sat in my car for a minute. This was a bad idea. I couldn't keep bothering my sister with my problems. Last year when I wasn't there for her when she needed me, she said I ran to her for all my problems, but I never returned the favor. She was right. I shouldn't be bothering her when she had a newborn and she and Nolan were still in the newlywed phase.

I was about to turn on my car and drive over to my apartment when the lights on the house flicked on. Avery opened the front door with Norah plastered on her hip.

"Come in already and tell me what's wrong!" she called to me.

I sighed and wiped my eyes again before getting out of the car.

When she saw me, her face fell. "Oh no, what happened?"

I burst into tears, and then Norah started crying, but my sister laughed. She walked inside, and I followed her into the living room. Nolan was at the brewery, so I felt like an ass for bothering my sister. She got Norah to settle down, and she gave me that look that told me I better talk.

The tears flowed down my face. "I'm sorry. I shouldn't be bothering you."

She handed me a box of tissues. "Tell me what's wrong."

"Felix."

"What about him?"

I dabbed at my eyes. "I fell in love with him."

Avery smiled, but it disappeared in an instant when she saw my pained expression. "Wait a minute. Why are you so upset?"

"Because I woke up this morning, and he was gone!"

She rocked Norah in her arms. "You better explain everything to me, because I don't understand."

I sighed and spewed out everything. I told her about the night of the thunderstorm and how I asked him to comfort me with sex. And how that turned into a fling. But I didn't want to let him go. By the end, I was a mess of tears and a snotty nose.

"Are you sure he didn't leave a note or something?" she asked.

I wiped my tears with the back of my hand. "Yes!"

She squinted at me in suspicion. "Did you look under the bed? Maybe it fell?"

"Well...no, but why didn't he answer my calls and texts?"

She bounced her crying baby in her arms as she thought. "I don't know. But maybe there's an explanation."

"Like what?" I cried.

She squeezed my hand. "Gem, I jumped to conclusions with Nolan. I don't want you to make the same mistakes, okay? How about you stay over tonight?"

I shook my head. "No. That's okay. I want to sleep in my bed tonight."

I didn't believe there was an explanation for why Felix left. I pushed him to stay, and he lied to me instead of telling me the truth. He promised not to break my heart, but I should have trusted my instincts. Felix Jameson was a Grade A asshole.

I stood up and brushed myself off. "I better get home. I'm tired."

Avery gave me the 'mom look,' like she knew I was lying. "Honey..."

"I'll see you later!" I called after her as I rushed out of her house. I didn't let her stop me. I left and drove over to my apartment, so I could wallow in my self-pity.

I sat in my bed and cried while I thought of how this hurt more than if Felix had told me he didn't love me. I checked my phone again, but there still wasn't a response. I tried him again, and it rang and rang until it went to his voicemail. I stabbed out an angry text to him and cried myself to sleep.

The next day, I waited until the brewery opened and walked over. I didn't say hello to any of my coworkers as they started their shifts. I went back into the office and found Declan sitting behind his desk. His eyes lit up as he saw me.

"There's my marketing director!"

I shook my head. "No."

His face fell. "What?"

I threw my apron down on his desk. "No, Declan. I'm done."

His brows knitted together. "I don't understand."

"I fucking quit, Dec. I'm done."

I didn't let him get in another word. Instead, I stormed out of the brewery and went home.

Was it foolish to turn down the marketing director job? Yes. Was it a bad idea to quit the brewery with no backup plan? Also yes. But I couldn't work side-by-side with the man who broke my heart three times. Maybe I could make a go at upping my sales in my jewelry store. Maybe that could be my next step.

I sat in my living room and took out my jewelry-making kit. Inside were some shells from the lake. Maybe I could add nautical jewelry, too, and diversify my inventory. Or I could find a different job. I should check if Sullivan's bar was hiring. Or I could move back to the city.

My phone beeped on the coffee table. I ignored the text from my sister. Felix hadn't responded to my 'go fuck yourself' text from last night. He had made it clear he didn't care about me. Maybe he never did and had been pretending all week long. I was just someplace to stick his dick in for a no-strings-attached fling and nothing else.

I wished I hadn't let my heart get in the way. I wished he had never told me why he stood me up. I couldn't hate him when I knew his reasons for keeping me away. It would have been nice if he had been honest with me instead.

I went to the Poconos to figure out what I wanted, but all I wanted was Felix. Instead, I came home with my heart shattered into a thousand tiny pieces.

CHAPTER TWENTY-SIX

FELIX

I woke the following day and felt hungover, but I wasn't. I fell asleep in the middle of the day, and when I checked my phone, I saw it was six a.m. the next morning. All that driving must have made me tired.

I checked my text messages, and my heart dropped into my stomach.

GEMMA: *Where are you?*

GEMMA: *???*

GEMMA: *What the fuck!! Where are you?*

GEMMA: *Fine, go fuck yourself then.*

FUCK!

I forgot to tell Gemma what happened with my sister. I meant to call her after I got Skye situated, and then I fell asleep. She must have woken up alone in bed and wondered where I was. She must have thought I cut and ran again.

I sighed and rubbed the sleep from my eyes. I couldn't believe I was so careless, and didn't at least leave a note for her. This wasn't the way I wanted our relationship to start.

It was too early for my sister to be awake, but I slept through dinner. I didn't know why she didn't wake me. Or worse, did she skip dinner because she couldn't get me to wake up? I felt like such a fuckup.

I went downstairs and was surprised to find my sister asleep on the couch. I definitely brought her upstairs last night. I made coffee and wracked my brain about how to fix things with Gemma. I stared at the angry text message and tried to type a response. I didn't blame her, but I didn't think she would answer me in a text. I had to go see her. I needed coffee and breakfast first.

I sipped my coffee and made French toast. I was cutting up fruit when Skye hobbled in on her crutches. "Sorry about last night, kiddo," I said to her. "How did you get downstairs?"

"Carefully," she muttered.

I put a slice of French toast on the serving plate and put another in the pan. "Why didn't you wake me?"

"I tried. You swatted me away."

I grimaced. "Sorry, half pint. All that driving made me tired. What did you do for dinner?"

"I made a frozen pizza. I can take care of myself every once and in a while, you know."

I finished making the French toast and divided up the slices on plates. I brought them over to the table and sat down across from my sister. She didn't speak as she ate, and neither did I, lost in thoughts about how to win back Gemma.

I shoveled food into my mouth and stared down at my phone. I clicked through my photos and to the ones of Gemma and me on the lake. She sent me the selfies she made me take with her that day, and I was glad she did, so I could remember how she made me feel. Gemma shone brightly, and her smile was like it was just for me. I felt like such an asshole for fucking it up so quickly.

"You look happy," my sister said.

I snapped my eyes up and glared at the nosy teenager staring down at my phone. "Nosy!"

She gave me a cute grin. "You love me!"

"Yeah, PITA, I do."

She tilted her head at me. "So, why do you look so sad today? Like someone peed in your cereal?"

I made a grossed-out expression. "Ew!"

"Fe-fe! What's wrong?"

I rubbed a hand across my beard. "I was so worried about getting to you, I forgot to tell Gemma where I was going."

She raised an eyebrow. "Did you text her?"

"My phone died, and then I forgot to call her last night."

She cringed. "Is she mad?"

I nodded.

She leaned back in her chair and had a guilty look on her face. I immediately went into concerned parent mode when her eyes welled up into tears. "It's all my fault," she cried.

I jumped up from my seat and bent down in front of her. I put my hands around her face. "Skye, listen to me. You're the most important thing in my life. You're always going to come first. Gemma knows that. You needed me. It's not your fault that I don't know how to communicate."

"Bu-but, I don't want you to give up your life for me!" she wailed again, and the tears fell in fat drops. "It's not your job to be my dad!"

"I know, kiddo, but I'm your big brother. I'm always gonna be there for you," I told her and wiped the tears away. "This isn't your fault."

"It's always my fault. You and Roger broke up because of me."

I sighed. "Not because of you, okay?"

"Yes! When Dad went to jail, you dropped everything because you felt like you had to be the replacement dad. I want my big brother to be happy, and I don't want to be the reason you're not."

I wiped more of her tears as they came again. I hated seeing Skye like this. I wanted my sister to be protected at all times. I didn't want her to think she was a burden. It was hard raising her on my own, but I would do it all over again if I had to.

"You're my sister. Family's first, always. It's not your fault. I left the cabin without telling Gemma where I was going. So she's mad at me right now. None of that's your fault, okay? That's on me."

"Okay..."

"It's not half pint. I've been afraid of a relationship since Dad went to jail again, but I want to try with Gemma. I spent the week getting to know her and...I really like her, and I think you would too."

"I never liked Roger," she admitted.

"Really?"

She nodded and wiped away the rest of her tears. "He was too stuffy. Gemma looks fun!"

I laughed. That was one way to describe the woman who lit up any room she walked into. When Gemma smiled, it was like the sunshine was shining down on you. Like it was wrapping you in a warm hug.

"How are you gonna fix it?" she asked.

I shrugged. "I need to talk to her in person. I'm gonna go to the brewery when it opens. You'll be okay without me for a bit, right?"

She rolled her eyes. "My leg's just broken. I'm fine. Sophia's gonna come over, anyway."

I ruffled her hair. "Okay, half pint."

We finished breakfast, and I unpacked my bags from the cabin. I smiled when a stray seashell poured out of my suitcase. It reminded me of that day on the lake with Gemma. How she had fit so perfectly in my arms, and how my heart wrenched in my chest when she looked so sad on the boat after telling me she didn't want the week to end. I hadn't wanted our week to end either. I just hadn't planned on my colossal fuck up so soon.

I wanted to call her, but I thought it was better to talk to her in person. If I called, she might tell me to fuck off again. By the time I left, Sophia had come over, so I was okay with leaving Skye alone. Maybe I babied her a little, but I worried about her dropping her crutches or falling on her injured leg if no one was around.

I walked over to the brewery, but I didn't see Gemma behind the bar when I walked inside. I went into the back to check the schedule pinned up outside of Declan's office. Gemma wasn't on it today. Or tomorrow. Or all next week.

What the fuck?

I was about to walk into the office where Declan sat staring intensely at his computer, but then Nolan stormed over to me, looking mad as hell.

"You!" Nolan pointed at me.

I pointed at my chest. "What about me?"

"You fucking know," Nolan snarled at me.

Nolan MacGregor was a grumpy guy. Gemma teasingly called him a 'grumpy bear,' but other than mild annoyance, I'd never seen him shake with rage at me. Declan looked up at the sound of his brother's voice.

"Get your asses in here and shut the door!" Declan called to us.

Nolan glared at me, and he bumped me with his shoulder as he went into the office.

He sat in a chair next to his younger brother, and they both sat there staring at me as if they were waiting for me to explain myself. I quirked up my eyebrow as I stared back at them.

"Shut the door. We gotta have some words," Nolan snarled again.

I shut the door and flopped down into the chair in front of Declan's desk.

"Is Gemma on the schedule at all?" I asked. "I need to talk to her."

"No, she fucking quit," Declan said. "You wanna tell me why?"

What? That didn't make any sense. Gemma said she was going to take the marketing director position. Why would she up and quit the brewery altogether?

I looked at both of them, and they were staring daggers at me. Nolan had his arms crossed over his chest.

"Felix, I like you," Nolan began. "But you fucked with my family, and I can't forgive that."

I held up my hands. "Whoa, wait a second. What are you talking about?"

Declan pointed at me. "You want to tell me why, after Gemma spent a week in the Poconos with you, she came into the brewery, tossed down her apron, and said she didn't want the marketing job? Not just the job, she quit the brewery entirely."

"You want to tell me why my wife called me in tears asking me to help her sister because she meddled when she shouldn't have, and Gemma's heartbroken?"

I sighed. "Fuck."

"Gemma might be a flighty pain in the ass, but she's ours, and she's family," Nolan said and glared at me. "Anyone who hurts my family can get fucked."

Declan put a hand on his brother's arm. "Easy, big guy. Felix, what happened?"

"I messed up. I came here to apologize to make it right."

"What did you do?" Nolan asked. He had his arms crossed over his big chest, clearly still pissed off at me.

"My sister broke her leg and called me in a panic. I didn't think I just went to her and didn't tell Gemma. By the time I realized what happened, my phone had died," I explained. I glared at the big guy. "You, of all people, should understand my sister always comes first."

He nodded and ran a hand through his beard. "Okay, okay, man, I get it. I do. She comes first."

Declan took off his glasses and rubbed the bridge of his nose. He shoved them back onto his face and stared at me, dumbfounded. "So...wait, Gemma quit because you're a dumbass who couldn't bother to wake her up and say, 'Gem, I have a family emergency.' How am I surrounded by dumbasses?"

That got him the double finger salute from me and his brother.

Nolan sighed. "Bro, sorry to go all aggro on you. When my wife's upset, it consumes me. I'm sorry Avs meddled. I told her she shouldn't have done that, but she just wants Gemma to be happy."

"We all do," Declan agreed. "I thought it would be better after you finally banged, but it got worse."

I raised an eyebrow.

Declan rolled his eyes. "Bro, we have security cams. I thought it was super weird that two of my best bartenders did a terrible job closing. Then I saw the footage of your tongue down her throat."

He shuddered and pretended to gag. That shouldn't have made me smile, but it did. I was glad Declan only ever saw Gemma as an annoying little sister.

"There's a camera in the supply closet?" I asked.

Declan shook his head. "Nah, but the hallway camera picks up things if the closet door is open."

I sighed. "I never thought I could have something real with her. Not when I have my sister to worry about."

Declan rolled his eyes. "No wonder you two martyrs get along. How old's your sister?"

"Thirteen."

"She doesn't need you to sacrifice everything for her," Declan said. "You can have a life and be a single dad, you know. I'm sure your sister wants that for you."

I nodded. "She does. I need to make this right with Gemma. She was gonna take the job."

"She was?" Declan asked.

I nodded.

"Oh, I know," Nolan said.

"You did?" Declan asked his brother.

Nolan ran a hand through his beard again. "Yeah, one of my buddies called me and said he met our marketing director at his brewery up in the Poconos. Talking about doing guest lines for each other."

"Why didn't you tell me?" Declan asked.

Nolan shrugged. "I figured that was Gemma's job, and she would handle it."

"The whole time she was at the cabin, all she thought about was the brewery," I said. "We toured breweries, and she said it was for research, not fun."

Declan sighed. "I know. That's why I changed all the passwords. I wanted her to think about her career."

I nodded. "She did. I'll fix this, but I have to get her to talk to me first."

Nolan nodded. "The Jensen Sisters can be stubborn. Believe me, I know. Gem will need some convincing."

"Right, this is a misunderstanding," Declan agreed. "Get Gem to see that."

I nodded. "I'm sorry about all this. I have to go find her."

I left the brewery and walked over to Gemma's apartment a couple of blocks away. I pounded on the door, but she never answered it. Maybe she wasn't home. I called her a few times, but it rang and rang. I even texted her, too.

ME: *Sweet thing, I'm so sorry. Please talk to me.*

I ended up going back home after a couple minutes of sitting on the steps of her porch. I only left when her neighbor in the duplex below her walked out on the porch to see what was going on.

When I got home, I saw a text from her.

GEMMA: *You didn't have to lie to me.*

ME: *Can we talk?*

GEMMA: *No.*

I sighed and went into my room while Skye and Sophia hung out in the living room. I didn't understand why Gemma wouldn't see reason. It was one minor mistake, but she wouldn't even let me apologize. I wasn't sure how I could make it right if she wouldn't talk to me.

I sat at my desk and worked on Gemma's logo. I knew she was going to love this design, even if she hated me and didn't want to be with me anymore. I finished it up and sent it to her with a note explaining what happened. I hoped she would come around if she knew the truth.

CHAPTER TWENTY-SEVEN

GEMMA

I took a swig of my Drakesville Lager and stared down at the email in my inbox.

Gemma,

Here's the logo for your shop. I hope you love it. I'm sorry about leaving without telling you. My sister needed me, and I wasn't thinking. I told you there would be times I'd disappoint you, and I'm sorry. Please, talk to me.

Love,

Felix.

Lies. All of it lies.

I couldn't believe him again, not when he had broken my heart so many times already. Maybe I made a mistake quitting the brewery, but I couldn't bear to see the man I loved every day when he shattered my heart.

Avery said I was being unreasonable, and it was just a misunderstanding. What did she know? She and her perfect lumberjack husband were having their happily ever after with their adorable baby. I'd never have that happiness. Felix Jameson cursed me and then broke my heart multiple times. And I let him.

I finished my beer and motioned for another from the bartender. I couldn't show my face at the brewery, so I was a block down the street at Sullivan's Bar. Kelly Sullivan, one of the owners, gave me a sympathetic look.

"Hun, how about I get you some water instead?" she asked.

I shook my head. "Nah. Another Drakesville Lager's good for me."

She gave me water instead. "Drink this, hun."

I grumbled but took the offered water. The room was spinning, so maybe she had a point.

"You hiring?" I asked.

She shook her head. "Sorry, Gem. We can barely pay our staff as it is."

I cocked my head at her. "Huh. Well, if you need a marketing revamp, I'm your girl. I was supposed to take a marketing director job, but I threw it all away."

"Yeah, how about you explain that one to me?" a deep voice asked from behind me.

I turned at the sound of Declan MacGregor's annoyed voice behind me. "Declan," I cheered. I was happy to see him, even though he didn't seem happy to see me. He glared at me from behind his black plastic-rimmed glasses.

"Hey, Declan," Kelly said to him.

He nodded. "Good to see you, Mrs. Sullivan."

The older woman gave him a smile. "It's been a long time, hun."

He nodded. "You know why."

She reached over the bar and squeezed his hand.

"You're still family, hun, even if you aren't with my daughter anymore."

I tilted my head and stared at Dec for a moment. I had never seen Declan with a girlfriend. I'd heard rumors about him, so I knew he wasn't celibate or anything. Like Nolan, Declan buried himself in his work, but I never knew why. He gave me a warning look, even though I wanted to ask so many questions. Kelly and her husband Sean had a daughter named Kelsey, but she was married with kids already, so that didn't make sense.

"Why are you here?" I asked instead.

Declan smoothed down an invisible wrinkle on his polo shirt. "Kelly called me and said you were drunk at her bar asking for a job."

I pinned a glare at the older woman, but she had moved on to serve a customer at the other end of the bar. I turned back to my brother-in-law. "Why did she call you?"

He sighed. "Believe me, this is the last place in all of Drakesville I ever wanted to step foot in again. She called Avery first, but she didn't answer."

I frowned. Of course, they called Avery first, so she could come and patronize me for being such a loose cannon. So she could 'mom' me like she always did.

"I want another beer," I muttered and played with the crystal around my neck.

"You've had enough," Declan said sternly.

I pouted.

He shook his head at that. I guess my pout only worked on Felix.

"Gem, why are you crying?"

I pressed a finger against my cheek and felt moisture there. Maybe I was a little too drunk because I hadn't even felt the tear. Thinking of Felix and how he broke me again made me come undone.

Declan offered me his hand, and I took it, but stumbled onto my feet. He rolled his eyes and led me out of the bar.

"I'm not walking your drunk ass all the way home. Crash on my couch tonight," he said and led me toward the brewery.

Declan lived above the tattoo shop a couple of doors down from the brewery in a tiny apartment. I think he just liked that it was so close to his work. I wanted to go home. I didn't want to crash on his couch, but it was getting harder to walk just the block to his apartment. I drank way more at Sullivan's than I'd realized.

Declan grunted at me as he helped me up the steps, and as soon as we got inside, I flopped down on the couch. He brought me a glass of water and sat down in the armchair with a look that told me to 'spill.'

"Why didn't you take the job?" he asked.

"I couldn't!" I groaned and sat up to gulp down the water. Okay, getting drunk by myself and having a pity party was a bad idea. I probably made a scene at the bar tonight too.

"Why?"

"Because I can't go back to working side-by-side with the man who broke my heart. My heart can't take it!"

Declan rubbed a hand across his clean-shaven jaw. His five o'clock shadow was coming in, and he looked annoyed. "Have you even talked to Felix? Did you let him explain what happened?"

"Sorta," I mumbled.

His email didn't explain everything, but I knew something had happened with his sister. I would have understood if an emergency came up, but the fact he didn't bother to tell me before he rushed off hurt. He warned me he would always choose her over me, and I thought I understood that, but I didn't. It hurt when I woke up and he was gone.

"Why don't you like to go to Sullivan's?" I asked, trying to change the subject.

He sighed. "Gem, I've only ever loved one woman in my entire life. She left for Stanford with my heart and never came back. That's why I don't like to go to Sullivan's. It hurts too much to be reminded of Lila."

"Then you understand why I can't work at the brewery."

He groaned. "You're being unreasonable."

"That's what Avery said," I scoffed.

"Because she's right. Will you please come back to work?"

I shook my head. "I can't."

"I'm not gonna fire Felix. He's our best bartender, and he's been with the brewery since the beginning. Go to sleep, and in the morning, fix things with Felix. You're both miserable, and you obviously miss each other. Stop being such a PITA."

I flopped back on the couch. "Was she really the only woman you ever loved?"

"Don't change the subject!"

"Tell me, Declan!"

"Annoying ass," he grumbled. "Lila Sullivan was my soul mate, but then she left and never came back. End of story."

"Not end of story!" I cried. "Tell me everything!"

"No, you PITA. Go the fuck to sleep and leave me alone."

"Or what?" I goaded him.

He groaned and got up from the couch. "Goodnight, Gemma!"

"No! Tell me!" I begged.

"You're so annoying!" he growled.

"Don't be a grumpy bear. That's Nolan's role. Is that why you're so uptight? You've gotten laid since her, right?"

He stared me down. "Of course I've gotten laid since then, but none of them have ever mattered to me. No spark or connection. It doesn't matter."

"Why not?"

He rubbed a hand across his jaw. "It just doesn't, Gem. Go to sleep."

"Night jerkface!"

I watched him give me the finger as he went into his bedroom.

I snickered to myself at his reaction. I drank more of my water and lay on Declan's couch, staring up at his ceiling. I must have been drunker than I thought if he had brought me here. Getting drunk alone in town was a bad idea. I should have done it in the comfort of my bedroom. At least Declan had central A/C in his tiny apartment. I don't know how he got so lucky with that. My apartment was always hot as balls.

I tried to go to sleep, but my mind was racing. I stared at my phone, but it hit me with the image of the background of me and Felix. I had changed it to the picture of us on the lake and never changed it when I came back to Drakesville. I was in that obnoxious hot pink bikini, and he was shirtless. He looked so hot, showing off his sleeve tattoos on the lake.

UGH! I shouldn't be thinking about him! I was mad at him for breaking my heart again. But I couldn't help how I still felt about him. And that sucked even more.

I felt the tears slide down my face. I'd blame it on being

a drunken hot mess, but it had been three days since Felix left me alone at the cabin and I was still crying myself to sleep every night. I should have walked out and drove home the moment I found Felix at my dad's cabin. I should have never gotten involved with him in the first place. I shouldn't have let him break my heart again.

CHAPTER TWENTY-EIGHT

FELIX

Gemma still wouldn't talk to me. It had been an entire week since we got back from the Poconos, and she wouldn't answer any of my calls or texts. Everyone at the brewery hated me now because they all loved Gemma, and she quit. It didn't take long for people to put two and two together.

I missed her. I missed her smile and the way she got excited when she thought about a marketing plan for the brewery. I missed her jumping up on the bed and begging me to go do something outdoorsy with her. I didn't expect her to be sleeping in my bed all the time when we got home, but I missed waking up beside her. Missed cuddling with her and stroking her hair. My chest ached at the thought that I couldn't be with her.

"Felix?" a voice called to me.

I snapped out of it and looked at my sister sitting on the couch beside me. "What's up?"

She eyed me with concern and pointed to the sketchbook in my hand. I looked down and realized I was drawing Gemma again. I was drawing the shape of her lips, the way they curved up into that sweet smile, and how her hair got into her eyes and made her look so cute. I drew those ocean-colored hues of her eyes too, and how they bored into your soul, like she knew every part of you.

"You keep drawing her," my sister said and shifted the ice pack on her broken leg.

I shut my sketchbook and tossed it on the other side of the couch. "Doesn't matter. What movie do you want to watch?"

"Fe-fe!"

"What?"

"Have you talked to Gemma?"

I shook my head. "She doesn't want to talk to me."

"But you miss her."

"Yeah, half pint, I do."

"Then you have to do something!" she insisted and waved her hands around.

"Like what?"

Her eyes got wide with excitement. "Like a big grand gesture! Like in all the romcoms and romance books I read. The hero always messes up, but then he does the big thing, and the heroine forgives him, and they have their HEA."

"Their what, now?"

"Happily Ever After! It's how all romance books end."

Romance books? Okay, I definitely needed to moderate her reading choices more closely.

"What type of romance books have you been reading?" I asked suspiciously.

"Nothing!" she squeaked.

Yeah, that nothing was a big something that she was hiding from me.

"Skye Anne."

She rolled her eyes. "I'm not a child, Felix! I know what sex is. I'm fine reading it. It's not something I want to do yet."

I sighed and calmed myself down. I didn't want to be the type of parent who shamed her for sex, even if I thought she was way too young to be reading books that depicted that. This was weird territory to be in.

"Okay, I'm just looking out for you. If...if that's something you think you're ready for, we can talk about it."

She made a face. "Gross, I don't want to talk about that with you. ANYWAY! You need to win Gemma back. Something to get her attention."

"Like what?"

She put a finger on her chin in thought. "First, try to apologize again."

"I did."

"And bring her flowers!"

"Hmm. I don't know what her favorite flower is."

"Get her sunflowers! They're the perfect summer flowers, and it's a sign of when you fell in love."

I ruffled her hair, and she gave me an annoyed look. "How do you know I'm in love?"

She rolled her eyes at me again. I bit my tongue from telling her that her face might stay like that if she kept doing it. That was a total dad thing to say.

"Because you've been so mopey! I hate it!" She stared at my sketchbook. "You should do something with those sketches."

"Like what?"

She shrugged. "I don't know. Make her a painting or something. Show her how much she means to you."

That wasn't a bad idea. Although I sent her the logo for

her shop and she never responded. I kept refreshing her shop too, and she hadn't updated it. I made the crystal logo perfect for her, and she wasn't using it.

I flipped through my sketchbook of all the sketches I did of us in the Poconos, and a plan started brewing in my head. I think I knew how I could win back Gemma.

I texted Declan.

ME: *Is there any availability in the loft? Maybe next month. I have an idea to get Gemma back.*

DECLAN: *Will she come back to the brewery if I say yes?*

ME: *That's the plan.*

DECLAN: *On it, let me move some things around.*

"Is it okay if Sophia comes over?" Skye asked.

"Sure. Text me if you need anything. I'm gonna be in the basement painting."

She looked excited at that. "Oh. What are you gonna do?"

"Paint my feelings," I said as I walked upstairs into my bedroom.

I changed into painting clothes, but before I went downstairs, I sat at my computer. I ordered a bouquet of sunflowers to be delivered to Gemma with a card. It bothered me that she wasn't giving me the chance to explain myself. I messed up by not giving a thought to her when my sister got injured. I understood why she was angry with me, but I wanted to make amends. I didn't stop loving Gemma when we left the Poconos, and I knew she didn't stop loving me.

I grabbed my paints and my sketchbook and headed down to the basement. I put my headphones on, grabbed one of the blank canvases, and put it on the easel. Spending time on my art at the cabin was the first time I created for my own enjoyment in a long time. A part of me had come alive when I was at the easel again. I got so busy taking care of my sister and being the provider that I didn't realize how much I missed working on my art for fun.

I opened my sketchbook and flipped to the sketch of the two of us on the dock together. I had my arms around her from behind, and I was kissing her temple as we looked out onto the water. It was so clear in my mind, the image of how we fit so perfectly together. And how I messed it all up by a simple mistake.

I drew on my easel and started to work. I was going to lose a lot of sleep over this, but I had to win her back. If not, having an art show in the loft would be a cool event for the brewery. It was a win-win for Declan.

I set up the last painting on the stand in the loft and looked back at my work. When I asked Declan to cut my hours, he didn't even question it. He shuffled the schedule around and had the new girl take more shifts while I spent the next month painting my ass off. I'd never painted this much in such a short time, but I hoped the lack of sleep was worth it.

"Wow, these are amazing," a feminine voice said from behind me.

I turned around and saw Avery MacGregor standing behind me, surveying my work. Of course, I enlisted Avery's help with the art show plan. She owed me for meddling.

"You think you can get her to come?" I asked.

She nodded. "I'll guilt-trip her into thinking it's for me so I can get out of the house."

I raised an eyebrow.

She laughed. "I've been stuck in my house for two

months with a newborn and an overprotective husband who's driving me batty. I'll get her to come."

"Thanks, Avs."

"She's being childish, so I want her to listen to you," she said as she walked around and surveyed the setup for the art show.

"I'm surprised Declan actually let me do this," I said.

"He wants his marketing director, so if you can win her back, he knows she'll reconsider quitting."

I laughed. "Oh, so there's something in it for him."

She laughed with me and stopped in front of the painting of Gemma and me on the dock. "This is my favorite."

"Mine too."

She tilted her head as she looked at it. "I'm glad I meddled. You two needed to figure it out."

I grimaced. "I did exactly what I said I was worried about. I chose my sister over her and didn't even think about her."

Avery squeezed my arm. "If you really love my sister, you'll figure it out. Gemma can be flighty and stubborn. Sorry, it's a family trait."

I laughed. "Thanks for your help. I want her to see that I'm sorry, that I want to try. I don't want us to be broken up."

"I know, honey. Don't worry. I'll get her up here, and she'll see what I see."

I nodded. I appreciated Avery's help, but I was still unsure. I'd find out tomorrow if all this work had been worth it or not. If I got Gemma back, or if I left with a broken heart.

CHAPTER TWENTY-NINE

GEMMA

*I*t had been a month since I got back from the Poconos, and I was still wallowing. I still didn't have a job, and I was barely selling anything in my shop. I could have used the new logo. It was amazing, but I didn't want to be reminded of Felix or how much he hurt me.

"Have you talked to him?" my sister asked.

"No," I muttered as I drank more beer from across her kitchen table.

"I think you're being unreasonable," she said.

I shook my head. "He told me he would choose his sister over me, but the fact I wasn't even a thought to him proved I was wrong about him."

"Gem, he made a mistake, and he's trying to own up to it. You should talk to him."

I shook my head.

"Will you at least take the job?"

"Avs! I can't go back there and have to see the man who broke my heart day after day."

"But you love the brewery!"

I loved the brewery and had been excited about starting my new career as the marketing director. It had also excited me that Felix and I were finally together. But then everything fell apart. Like it was the universe's way of telling us it wouldn't work out. I should have listened to Felix when he said we could only have a summer fling. Having something real with him just wasn't possible.

Avery frowned at me. "Look, there's a cool art show event at the brewery today. We should go."

I quirked an eyebrow at her. "An art show?"

That didn't sound like something Nolan and Declan would go for. That was the sort of event I would have pushed them to do. They would have grumbled about it and only agreed to it to get me to shut up. Who's idea was that?

Avery showed me her phone to show me the promo post on the brewery's Instagram account. I wanted to sigh because it looked like April posted that. She didn't even use hashtags again. How would people even know about it if we didn't have visibility on the platform outside of our followers?

"Let's go!" Avery urged.

"Why?"

"Because I've been cooped up in the house with the baby for two months, and I need to get out!"

I sighed. "Fine."

She grinned at me, and I should have been suspicious of her motives. I finished my beer while she got the baby situated. Nolan was already at the brewery, so Avery put Norah in her stroller, and we walked out of the house.

I didn't want to go to the brewery, but if my sister needed to get out of the house, I'd appease her. I still felt bad about not being there for her last year when she needed me. I think she knew it too, so I couldn't fault her for guilt-tripping me today.

"Hey, I heard Sullivan's might sell," she said as we walked down the street.

"Really?" I asked, but it didn't surprise me. I vaguely remembered asking for a job, but Kelly Sullivan said they couldn't afford to hire anyone else. That bummed me out. Sullivan's was a staple in Drakesville.

She nodded. "Kelsey, their oldest daughter, is a history teacher at the school with me. She said her parents are getting too old to do it, and she and her husband can't afford to take over. Her sister lives in California and is getting married soon, so it doesn't seem like they can keep it in the family."

"Oh no."

Avery frowned. "I know."

"Poor Declan!"

She pinned me with a confused look. "What about him?"

"Lila Sullivan's his one true love, and he's still pining over her."

Avery stopped the stroller and gave me a fascinated look. "Oh my god, tell me everything! Nol let it slip that he's worried about Dec's 'revolving door' of women."

"Ask Declan! That's all I got out of him. That's such a bummer about the bar, though. They could play up their classic Irish bar thing. We could do—" I cut myself off. I was already thinking about cross-marketing promotions, and that wasn't my job.

Avery smiled at me as we got to the door of the brewery. I narrowed my eyes at her because she brought it up on purpose.

She gave me a small smile while I held the door open for

her so she could push the stroller inside. She was swallowed up by Nolan, who almost immediately took Norah out of her stroller and held her to his chest. Avery folded up the stroller and handed Nolan the baby sling, so he could wear Norah on his chest.

"Hey, Gem," Nolan greeted once he had Norah on his chest. He looked so cute with the little baby cuddled up against him.

"You agreed to an art show?" I asked.

He nodded, but he looked like he was up to something. I was immediately suspicious. He jerked his chin up to the loft space upstairs. "Go look, let me say hello to my wife."

I gave him a dubious look as he kissed my sister. I cautiously walked up the steps into the loft space and stopped dead in my tracks when I reached the top.

There were paintings set up on display easels upstairs against the railing, and every single one of them was of me. Except for the one in the center, which was the sunset Felix had painted while we were at the cabin together.

Avery and Nolan had been up to something, after all.

I walked up to the first painting and stared back at the image of myself sitting on the dock with my feet in the water. My eyes were closed as I felt the afternoon sun on my face. I laughed at the next one depicting me chopping wood for the fire. I stared at the sunset painting, flashes of memories of my time with Felix running through my brain. Of all the kisses and apologies and broken promises. The next one looked like the selfie I had taken of us on the lake on the day I knew I had fallen for him.

When I moved over to the last painting, the butterflies climbed up my stomach. We stood on the dock in profile, looking out onto the water. Felix had his arms around me from behind, kissing my temple. I was wearing the black dress with pink flowers that matched my hair, while he was in a nice button-down shirt and looked hot as hell.

We looked so deeply and desperately in love, and I didn't understand why all the paintings at this 'art show' were of me. What was Felix playing at?

"He worked so hard on these," a small voice squeaked beside me, making me jump.

I turned to see a petite pre-teen girl with dark hair standing beside me on crutches. How did she even get up the steps?

"Excuse me?"

"It's all my fault," she told me.

I furrowed my brow at this strange girl. "What is?"

"I'm sorry, Gemma, it's all my fault." She gestured to the cast on one of her legs. "I broke my leg and wanted my brother, and he didn't even think to leave you a note. Because he's a dumbass!"

Wait, what? Her brother?

"SKYE!" Felix's voice scolded from behind me.

I turned around and saw Felix standing in front of me. He looked nice in a black button-down shirt and matching black jeans. His beard was neatly trimmed with his hair brushed back out of his face, like he had put in the effort to impress me. He held a bouquet of sunflowers in his hands. Just like the ones he sent to me weeks ago with an apology note. I had been so angry; I threw them both in the trash.

Skye grinned at Felix. "Well, you are!"

I turned back to the paintings in front of me. My heart fluttered at the last one again. Of how we fit so perfectly. And god, how I missed him. I missed the feel of his lips on mine and his arms wrapped around me. Of how he smiled at my excitability and never once berated me for my flaws. Or scolded me like my sister did for being such a flighty, immature asshole. Felix accepted all of me, and I had been so stubborn to not even listen to his apology.

I turned back around and crossed my arms over my chest. "Explain yourself. What's all this?"

"It's his grand gesture!" Skye explained. "He put his heart and soul into this to win you back."

I couldn't help the corner of my lips turning up into a small smile at how his sister was in his corner. It was obvious she loved him very much, and her going to bat for him might have softened my rock-hard heart.

Felix shot her a glare, but she just grinned at him. I held in the laugh when I saw him mouth "PITA" at her.

"Is he forgiven yet?" Skye asked.

"I don't know," I said with a sigh.

"Please!" she begged. "I don't want my big brother to be a boring monk for the rest of his life. He misses you, and I know you miss him, too."

I cocked an eyebrow at her. "How do you know that?"

"Because of the smile on your face when you looked at the paintings. Especially that last one. That's like romance book cover-worthy."

This girl was pulling hard for her brother, and I could appreciate that, but my fragile heart was still afraid of being hurt again.

Felix stepped in front of me and handed me the bouquet. "You wouldn't talk to me, so I needed to get your attention somehow. Skye said I needed to grovel."

I fingered a petal of one of the flowers but wouldn't look at him. If I looked into those dark eyes, I would cave. "Then grovel."

"I didn't want to leave you. I woke up to my sister calling me crying, and I immediately went into dad mode."

Skye nodded solemnly, confirming his story.

"I'm so sorry, Gemma. I never meant to hurt you. All I could think about was getting to Skye and making sure she was okay. I drove all the way to Cape May, and my phone died. By the time we got back to Drakesville, and I got her situated, I was beat. I passed out and then woke up to your 'go fuck yourself' message."

I cringed. That made me seem like such a bitch. He had been so focused on his sister, and I loved that about him, but it hurt that he hadn't even thought to wake me up to tell me what was going on.

"You made me feel like garbage. Like I meant nothing to you."

He grabbed my hand and kissed the bi pride heart on the inside of my wrist. A part of me wanted to recoil, to slap his hand away, but the part of me who still loved him, who missed him with every fiber of my being, was warming up. "I know, sweet thing. I understand if you don't want to take me back. I'm so sorry. I let you down almost immediately."

"I told you he's a dumbass!" Skye cut in.

"Hush you," Felix snapped at her.

I couldn't help the smile spreading across my face. Okay, she was a cute secret weapon to use against me. It was so sweet how she wanted to help her brother.

I looked back at the painting again and chewed on my lip. We were so happy up in the Poconos together. We looked so in love, and my heart yelled at me to give him another chance. To give him a thousand more chances. Because relationships were hard, but when someone loved you despite your flaws and they were baring their soul to you, it was a good idea to listen.

When I turned back around, he looked so sincere, like he knew he fucked up. And his sister gave me those pleading puppy dog eyes I couldn't say no to. But more than that, it was the fact he was laying out all his cards for me that made my heart win over my stubborn head.

"I would've gone with you. Or understood why you had to go. All I ask is that you don't keep me in the dark again. I get Skye's your world, but I want a piece of that, too."

"What are you saying?" he asked, confusion marring his handsome face.

"Do you forgive him?" Skye asked.

When I looked at his paintings, I felt the love he poured out onto the canvas. I felt his sincereness in knowing he fucked up. But I fucked up, too. Maybe I was stubborn by not giving him the chance to explain himself. I acted too rashly, thinking the worst of him, without letting him tell me he was sorry.

I nodded.

"Really?" Felix asked.

"I'm sorry, too."

"What are you sorry for?"

"For being my typical stubborn self. For not giving you a chance to apologize."

"Geez, just kiss already and get it over with!" Skye teased.

I yelped when Felix pulled me flat against his chest and slanted his mouth on mine. I dropped my flowers on the floor while he kissed me. I had missed the way he kissed me, like I was the only woman in the entire universe.

"GET A ROOM!" someone yelled. I was pretty sure it was one of the MacGregors. Assholes.

Felix pulled away from me with a laugh. He pressed his forehead against mine. "Gemma, I love you. I didn't mean to fall in love with you in the Poconos, but I did. I can't promise I won't be a dumbass again, but I'll try my best not to hurt you ever again. You're my sunshine."

I gave him another quick kiss. "I can't believe you did all these paintings and organized this."

"It was worth it. You're worth it."

"How did you know sunflowers are my favorite?" I asked.

"I didn't. Skye recommended them."

A smile spread across my face. That girl was so in her brother's corner, and I loved her already. I cupped Felix's bearded face. "I can't promise I won't be a stubborn, immature asshole again, but I'll try to be better. Losing you felt like my heart shattered into a million little pieces. And I don't want to feel that way ever again."

"I'm in it for the long haul, sweet thing."

"You're forgiven," I said. I leaned up against his ear. "But maybe you need to use your tongue ring on me a couple of times to really make up for it."

He laughed. "Such a brat."

My smile went from ear to ear. "Your brat."

"Damn fucking straight."

"Thanks for fighting for me."

"I'll always fight for you."

"That's all I can ask for."

"Tell me you're my girl for good."

I smiled at him, but instead of answering, I wrapped my hands around the back of his neck and pulled him down for another panty-melting kiss. He kissed me back like no one else was watching. Like we couldn't hear our siblings hollering in the background. We kissed like we were the only two people in the entire world, and I melted into the embrace of the man I loved.

EPILOGUE

FELIX

FOURTH OF JULY WEEKEND THE FOLLOWING YEAR

"*A*re we there yet?" Skye whined from the backseat of my car.

Gemma laughed in the passenger seat at my sister's question. In the backseat, Skye and Sophia giggled with each other. Not sure why I agreed to take the two rambunctious teens with us up to the cabin for the holiday weekend. I owed the Parks for always taking my sister to Cape May each year, so maybe I deserved this.

"Not yet, kiddos!" Gemma told them, looking back at them with a smile.

I smiled to myself as I drove down the drive toward the cabin. We were almost there, just a few more minutes. When I asked Gemma if she wanted to spend the Fourth of July weekend at the cabin, she had no idea I had ulterior motives or what I had planned today.

But my sister did. That was why she asked to come with me. She wanted to see the look on Gemma's face when I asked her to be my wife. I loved my sister, but Skye was nosy as shit.

Gemma and I had been together about a year now, and like any relationship, it wasn't perfect. There were times I didn't tell her things or when she overreacted, but instead of letting her run, we worked through it. It helped that my sister adored her, and the feeling was mutual.

The brewery was thriving with Gemma at the marketing helm. After the pop-up art show in the loft space, it gave her an idea for the Arts Fest. We ended up having the loft used as a pop-up art shop and then had our regular booth in the town square. It did really well, and the MacGregors were happy with how organized Gemma was with the business. She was amazing at it, and with her help, my design business was doing awesome. I was selling my paintings occasionally, too.

"What do you do up here?" Sophia asked.

"The same as Cape May," I said to her.

"I can teach you girls how to fish," Gemma said. "And build a campfire. I'll take you out on the boat, and we'll cruise around the lake. We can swim in the lake or kayak. There's so much stuff to do!"

I smiled. "You know Gem, she's go-go-go."

"You love it," Gemma teased.

I grabbed her hand and kissed the back of her palm. "I do."

"Ew!" Sophia and Skye teased at our public display of affection.

I let Gemma's hand go and pulled up into the driveway next to Nolan's car.

Gemma gave me a suspicious look. "Wait, did I read the calendar wrong?"

"Nope."

She started calculating stuff in her head. "Okay, so Nolan, Avery, and the baby will take the primary bedroom, we'll take my room, and the girls can have the guest room. Or the pull-out sofa."

I cut the engine and leaned over to give her a quick kiss. "Sweet thing, relax."

The girls ran out of the car without helping bring the stuff in, but we laughed it off. It was around dinnertime, and Nolan was grilling on the porch. He waved to us as we brought all our stuff inside. Avery was inside with the baby and her dad.

She gave me a big hug when she saw me. "Ready?" she whispered in my ear.

I nodded.

No, that was a lie. I wasn't ready to propose to Gemma. The engagement ring was burning a hole in my pocket, but I was afraid she'd say no. I wanted Gemma to be mine forever. She moved in with us last month after months of not staying at her apartment. It felt like the right course of action. We were on the same page with everything, but I was still nervous.

"Dad!" Gemma cried. "I didn't know you were coming. Shit, where are we gonna fit everyone?"

"The girls can take the sofa. They're young," I said. "Stop worrying about it."

"We're good, sweetheart," her dad said, and he gave me a big smile.

I asked her dad for his blessing last week, and he laughed in my face and told me not to tell Gemma I did that.

Then we watched a Phillies game together and bemoaned about how boring baseball was and how we couldn't wait until hockey season was back. Her dad was pretty chill, and I understood Gemma more after getting to know him better.

"Do you need help with dinner?" Gemma asked her sister.

Avery waved her hand. "Nope. Nolan's got the grill going, and I'm working on the mac and cheese and vegetables. We're good." She reached into the fridge and grabbed two Drakesville Lagers for us. "Here, take a load off and have a drink before dinner."

Gemma eyed her sister with suspicion but took the beer.

The girls were outside, sitting down by the fire pit, gossiping. Skye and Sophia were getting into that phase of chasing boys, and I was up to my eyeballs in worry. Gemma laughed at me and reminded me of how she was at that age. That didn't make me feel any better.

"Let's go down to the dock," I said to Gemma as I sipped on my beer.

"Okay."

We walked down to the dock, and Gemma sipped her beer while she looked out over the water. Her hair was freshly dyed hot pink again, and she was wearing a strappy white dress with sunflowers on it. She looked like summer, and the way she smiled at me was like the sun shining down on me.

"What's with you?" she asked.

"Huh?"

She raised an eyebrow. "You're being mad weird today. What's up?"

That was my cue. I got down on one knee. Her mouth

was agape as I held open the ring box to her. "Gemma, will you marry me?"

"Wait, for real?" she asked.

"Yes, for real!"

She put her hands to her chest. "Wait, is that a moonstone?"

"For a new beginning because I want a new life with you as my wife."

She stared down and then glared at me. "Oh my god, you planned this entire weekend! That's why my family's here!"

I laughed. "Yeah, sweet thing. I wanted to do it where we fell in love, right here at the cabin. So what do you say?"

"Oh. Oh yes, duh!" she exclaimed.

I slid the ring on her finger and stood up. She admired the ring, and the sunlight hit the rainbow reflections of the gemstone on her hand. When I thought about proposing, I knew a regular diamond wasn't good enough for my girl. My girl loved her crystals, and the moonstone one felt right for her.

"It's perfect," she told me. "I absolutely love it, and I love you."

"I love you too."

"C'mere," she purred, pulling me into her arms.

I slanted my mouth on hers and kissed her in the place we first fell in love. With the sun setting behind us and our family cheering from the cabin, it was like the universe was telling us everything was going to be alright. Gemma Jensen was my sunshine, and I couldn't wait to spend the rest of my life with her.

ACKNOWLEDGMENTS

I am so excited that this book is finally out in the world. Writing my first couple where both of them were bisexual was such a journey. Especially since Gemma and Felix didn't tell me that until I started writing their book. This is one of my favorite books I've written, and I hope you all love it too.

Big thanks to my betas on this one—Chris, Jlynn, and Kat. I appreciate all of your feedback. Special thanks to my critique partners as well. I was really worried about this book, so your support and encouragement were just what I needed.

Another thanks goes to my editors who helped me bring this book to life. Big props to Leah Francic for helping me through the big picture developments edits, and to Kate Seger for doing the line and copy work. I appreciate your comments and guidance to make this book shine.

Thanks as always goes to my readers for the support and your love of my books. I couldn't do this without you.

Also I have to shoutout my book designer, Emily from Emily's World of Design. I think I tortured you a little with this one, but the final outcome is one of my favorite covers!

There will be one more book in this series, so look out for Declan and Lila's book, Temporarily In Love coming soon!

TEMPORARILY IN LOVE
SNEAK PEEK

LILA

END OF SEPTEMBER

I always forgot what fall in Pennsylvania was like. The leaves turned color almost overnight, and the air got chilly enough that all you needed was a light jacket and a cup of hot cider. Maybe it was my imagination, but the town almost smelled of cinnamon and pumpkin, like it was teasing me for being gone for so long.

In California, you could find hipsters with big bushy beards wearing flannel and girls sipping on pumpkin spice lattes, but it wasn't the same as fall in Drakesville, Pennsylvania. Having lived on the other side of the country since college, my memory of what an East Coast fall looked like had slipped away.

When I walked up into the town square for the annual Arts Fest with my sister and her kids, fallen leaves crunched beneath my boots, reminding me of how much I loved this season. I marveled at how pretty the trees looked, painted in shades of red, yellow, and orange. If you've ever wanted to see how gorgeous autumn could be in my home state, come to Drakesville and see for yourself.

I pulled my plaid jacket around myself and shivered at the autumn air hitting me in the face. That prompted a laugh from my sister, Kelsey. "It's like sixty degrees. How are you cold?"

"This is cold for me!" I argued.

She laughed and shook her head as she held her toddler on her hip. "You've been in California too long. It's perfect weather for the Arts Fest."

My niece Callie babbled on my sister's hip as my other niece Cora clasped my hand and stomped on the leaves with me. My sister hadn't been happy about me encouraging that behavior. But how could you enjoy fall if you couldn't jump into the leaves?

I hadn't been back to town for my favorite season in years. I barely made it back for Thanksgiving or Christmas. Part of that was because I worked a demanding job as an intellectual property lawyer for a big tech company. The other part was that I actively avoided coming home at all costs. I'd do anything to avoid running into Declan MacGregor.

But when you caught your fiancé sleeping with his secretary and your mom called, saying your dad wanted to sell the family bar, you got your ass on a plane home to sort it all out.

Sullivan's Bar was a staple in our town, and I couldn't bear the thought of my dad selling it. So many things in town had changed since I left for Stanford. I didn't want the bar to be yet another one of those things.

Dad didn't want to talk about it when he picked me up from the airport last night. Instead, he kept asking me if I had set a date for my wedding. I hadn't told my family Chad and I had broken up yet. Or that I had quit my job because of it.

"Auntie Lila, can we get cookies from the bakery?" my niece asked, snapping me out of my thoughts.

"Ask your mommy," I said.

My sister frowned.

Cora was already hopped up on sugar because I was the fun aunt. That's what Kels got for berating me about being thirty-four with no babies of my own. I thought I'd have that soon, but a part of me was glad I never settled on a wedding date. Maybe deep down, I always knew it wasn't going to work out with Chad.

We hadn't been in a good place in a long time. When he proposed, I only said yes because I thought I was running out of time and options. I wanted a family, but my techie fiancé never made time for me, and we worked in the same damn building. Sure, he had more pressure on him as the CEO, but I worked the same soul-sucking hours. His cheating on me was only half the reason I sent in my resignation and headed home to Pennsylvania.

"Cora, no. You'll spoil your dinner," my sister warned and shot me a glare.

I ruffled Cora's red hair. "Sorry, kiddo. Hey, let's go over to the tattoo booth and get you a temporary tattoo."

Cora practically dragged me over to the booth. The tattoo shop, Tattooed Mamas, was female-owned, which I loved, and earlier, they were giving out temporary tattoos for the kids. It would distract Cora for a while.

"Hey, you!" Lizzie called out to me as we approached. We had been friends since high school, and while she still had the colorful lavender hair, now her body was painted with the ink of her profession. "Lila Sullivan, as I live and breathe."

I frowned. "As you live and breathe, really Liz?"

She shrugged. "I could have said, 'hey youse guys' instead, but I don't think you remember what it's like living in the Philly area anymore."

"Har har har. I still pronounce water 'wooder.' I didn't forget my roots," I said.

She laughed. "What was the first thing you did when you got to town?"

"Ate one of my dad's cheesesteaks!"

"What? You didn't stop at Pat's or Geno's on your way back from the airport?"

I scoffed. "What am I? A tourist?"

We laughed together. Pat's and Geno's were nowhere near the airport, but it was a joke we always made when I came to town. Only tourists who went to South Street went there.

Lizzie's eyes darted to my niece. "Hey, Cora. You want a tattoo?"

My little niece nodded. Lizzie smiled and brought Cora over to a chair behind the booth. Lizzie made a big production of putting the temporary tattoo on my niece's arm. She was good with kids like that, and I had a feeling she often did this with her own.

When it was done, Cora was all smiles and skipped over to me to show me the rainbow-colored butterfly tattoo on her bicep.

"Wow, look at that. Did that hurt?" I asked.

"Nope! I'm a big girl!" Cora said proudly.

I smiled at her and smoothed down her hair. "Yes, you are. Now, what do you say to Lizzie?"

"Thank you!" she told my friend.

Lizzie smiled at me. "Hey! You should come to the brewery later to get a beer with me after the fest."

I made a face.

I had no intention of ever stepping foot in the MacGregor Brothers Brewing Company. It might be a block away from my family's bar, and people raved about their beers, but I wasn't welcome there. And for good reason, too.

"You still haven't gone there?" Lizzie asked.

I shook my head.

"Lila, that was in high school. I'm sure Declan's over your breakup by now. It's been like fifteen years."

Sixteen, but who was counting? Oh right, me. Because I wasn't over the breakup with my high school sweetheart. I wasn't sure I ever could be. Even though I was the one to break up with him.

Every relationship since had failed because my heart only had room for Declan freaking MacGregor. It explained why when I found Chad with his secretary, I simply took off my engagement ring and placed it on his desk. I didn't even say anything to him. I sent him a formal email the next day informing him I was going out of town and wanted his stuff out of my house. If I had loved Chad, I wouldn't have done that. But I left my heart in Drakesville long ago, and it was the reason I avoided coming back. It hurt too much.

"Think about it!" Lizzie said.

"We better go." I waved at her while I walked with my niece to find my sister.

Unfortunately, Kelsey was exactly where I didn't want her to be. I found her standing in front of the brewery's booth, talking to a tall woman with pink hair and flower tattoos on her arm. The pink-haired lady looked excited and gestured wildly with her hands. I didn't recognize her, but she looked younger than me, so we probably never passed each other in school. Drakesville was a small town, but despite what Hallmark or the Gilmore Girls told you, you didn't know everyone and their business when you lived here.

Cora ran over to her mom, and my sister pretended to be wowed by the temporary tattoo on her daughter's arm. Kelsey was a good mom; at least she gave my parents some grandkids. My biological clock was ticking, and I didn't see that being an option for me anytime soon.

"Look who it is!" a big, booming voice said behind me.

I spun on my heel and came face-to-face with Nolan MacGregor.

He looked older than I remembered. He still had that big bushy beard, and coupled with his red plaid shirt, he looked like a burly lumberjack—like a husky Brawny Man. I scanned him, then narrowed my eyes when I noticed the baby strapped to his chest. The last I heard, Nolan and his wife divorced a couple of years ago. But maybe she had a change of heart, and that was a rumor.

"Hi, Nolan," I sighed.

"He's not around. He's doing spreadsheets," he said, fixing me with a warning glare. "And you better stay away."

"Excuse me?"

This wasn't the first time Nolan told me to piss off. The last time I saw him, I ran into him the next town over at the super grocery store, and he told me not to bother Declan while I was in town. Nolan was nothing if not fiercely protective of his little brother.

"You heard me, Lila. Stay away from my brother. He doesn't need you opening up that old wound again."

I couldn't ask Nolan what he meant because the baby on his chest started to cry. Nolan's scowl increased, but he took her out of the sling and rocked her. Watching the big bear of a man gently soothe his daughter was cute.

"Oh, there you are." A dark-haired petite woman with curves came up behind Nolan. She took the baby from his arms. "Aw, Peanut, be good for Daddy."

Okay, he definitely didn't have a baby with his ex-wife Kath. I didn't recognize the woman beside him, but she might not be a townie. She noticed me for the first time and gave me a sheepish look as she put the baby on her hip. "I'm sorry. Where are my manners? I'm Avery MacGregor. I don't think we've been introduced."

She held out her hand to me and we shook hands. "Lila Sullivan."

Her blue eyes lit up. "Oh! You're Kelsey's sister. We teach at the high school together." Avery saw me staring at her baby. "Do you want to hold her?"

"Oh. Can I?"

She nodded. "But fair warning, she likes to pull hair."

"And beards," Nolan muttered.

I smiled at that. It was good to know the more things changed in this town, the more they stayed the same, like Nolan MacGregor being a grump. Avery put the baby in my arms, who immediately tried to pull on my hair. I laughed and shook my long chestnut locks out of the way.

Avery chuckled. "Do you have kids? Seems like you have practice with this."

I shook my head as I held her baby, and my heart did a somersault at how she laid her little head on my chest and curled up into me.

"What's her name?" I asked.

"Norah," Nolan grunted.

"Oh," I sighed, and my heart panged at the memory of Norah MacGregor. "Oh, Nol, you're such a softie."

Avery beamed. "Yeah, he is."

Nolan scowled, but when Avery reached up on her tiptoes and gave him a kiss, a smile spread across his face. Kath never made him smile like that. I don't remember the last time I saw Nolan MacGregor smile. I could tell he loved his wife something fierce. And he had a baby. He looked so happy, and I never thought the grouch of a man would look like that.

"I can't believe you have a baby," I said.

Avery took Norah out of my arms as she started to fuss.

"I can't believe you showed your face in town again," Nolan shot back.

Avery arched an eyebrow at her husband. I wasn't about to tell her that her husband hated me because of what I did to his brother.

"Lila!" my sister called out to me, distracting me from the conversation. She walked over to me with a plastic cup of beer in her hand. "Here, have a beer," she said and handed it to me.

I wrinkled my nose. "No, thanks."

"It's a pumpkin beer. You love pumpkin," said a voice from behind me. A deep manly voice that I was hoping I'd never hear ever again.

Crap. This was why I never came home.

You can find the full book HERE

ALSO BY DANICA FLYNN

PHILADELPHIA BULLDOGS

Take The Shot

Score Her Heart

Against The Boards

The Chase

MACGREGOR BROTHERS BREWING COMPANY

Accidentally In Love

Temporarily In Love

ABOUT THE AUTHOR

Danica Flynn is a marketer by day, and a writer by nights and weekends. AKA she doesn't sleep! She is a rabid hockey fan of both The Philadelphia Flyers and the Metropolitan Riveters. When not writing, she can be found hanging with her partner, playing video games, and reading a ton of books.

www.ingramcontent.com/pod-product-compliance
Lightning Source LLC
Chambersburg PA
CBHW071242190726
48292CB00007B/2384